THE HEADLESS HORSEMAN RIDES AGAIN

Ichabod Crane wasted no time getting to the heart of the matter: "So. Three persons murdered. Is anyone suspected?"

"Constable," Baltus Van Tassel said indulgently, "how much have your superiors explained to you?"

"Only that the three were slain in open ground and their heads found severed from their bodies—"

"The heads were not found severed," Reverend Steenwyck interrupted. "The heads were not found at all."

"The heads are gone?" Ichabod asked.

"Taken." Notary Hardenbrook leaned forward. "Taken by the Headless Horseman. Taken back to hell."

Sleepy Hollow

Including the classic story by Washington Irving

A novelization by Peter Lerangis
Screen story by Kevin Yagher and Andrew Kevin Walker
Screenplay by Andrew Kevin Walker
Based upon the story by Washington Irving

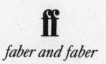

faber and faber

An Archway Paperback first published in the USA by
POCKET BOOKS, a division of Simon & Schuster Inc.
1230 Avenue of the Americas, New York, NY 10020
First published in Great Britain in 2000
by Faber and Faber Ltd, 3 Queen Square
London WC1N 3AU

™Paramount Pictures.

Book design by Jaime Putorti
Printed in Great Britain by Mackays of Chatham plc, Chatham, Kent

A CIP record for this book is available from the British Library

ISBN 0-571-20585-2

10 9 8 7 6 5 4 3 2

CONTENTS

SLEEPY HOLLOW

PROLOGUE

October 1799.
Sleepy Hollow, New York.
To the New York City Constabulary:
Three murders. Need help. Respond immediately.

B. Van Tassel

It was the most recent of many messages. Each had been more desperate than the one before.

Each, of course, had been completely ignored.

No one in the police department had heard of Sleepy Hollow.

Nor, presumably, had anyone else in the city.

To a New Yorker, for all intents and purposes the world ended at Wall Street. One seldom ventured north into the farmlands and swamps of Manhattan Island, let alone over the river to the gentle acreage named for a family known as the Broncks.

Sleepy Hollow, a two-day journey farther, might as well have been the moon.

What some judged aloofness, New Yorkers called necessity. The city was growing too fast to control. Distant murders held little shock value in a place where death was a daily event. Where streets were littered with victims of passion and pettiness, of debts and grudges held too long. Where yellow fever wiped out thousands, poverty ran rampant, and social services consisted of sixteen constables and forty marshals, three jails, a workhouse, and a poorhouse.

In New York, just as in Sleepy Hollow, a wily killer could pull off a perfect crime—because in 1799 the dead did not tell secrets.

If life was a raw and unforgiving public journey, death was a solemn mystery best handled by family and church. A victim who had no kin became a disposal problem for the state. The body was of no use. It held no clues.

Unless one knew how to look for them.

1

HE WAS DEAD. NO DOUBT ABOUT THAT.

His head bobbed on dark and brackish water, his hair floating among the debris like a weary, lost animal.

A drowned river rat, Constable Ichabod Crane had thought at first.

Perhaps he should have left it at that, but something about the object had stopped him: the languid movement, the suggestion of weight underneath the hair.

Approaching the edge of the Hudson River, Ichabod Crane swallowed hard. At times such as these, he wished he didn't see so much.

It was his nature, for better or worse. He carried himself with an edge of caution, a sharp and suspicious eye, and a healthy disrespect for normal police procedure. That made him, among his fellow New York City constables, either the most innovative or the most annoying man on earth.

As Ichabod leaned over the pier, his lantern's light revealed an outline below the surface of the river: a body—male.

With his free hand, he rang his alarm bell as hard as he could.

Footsteps echoed from the cobbled streets behind him. "Where are you?" a voice rang out.

"Over here!" Ichabod shouted. Looking over his shoulder, he saw two familiar silhouettes emerge into the light of a streetlamp—Constables Green and Witherspoon. "I need your help with this!"

Ichabod set down his alarm bell and reached underwater, hooking his arm under the body's shoulders.

"Constable Crane—Ichabod Crane?" came Green's wary voice. "Is that you?"

The body was heavy, unbelievably heavy. Ichabod planted one foot firmly against a wood piling to keep from falling in. "None other," he grunted. "And not only me. I have found something."

The body emerged from the murk. Straining against the weight, Ichabod dragged it onto the dock. Its face was a swollen caricature, a balloon image of a man. Its clothes strained against the bloat of a waterlogged torso. Ichabod forced himself to breathe deeply, to avoid an overpowering wave of nausea.

"I have found something which was lately a man," Ichabod told the other officers.

Even in the darkness, Ichabod could see the faces of his two colleagues. Green murmured something about a wheelbarrow, and then they were gone.

How did this happen? Ichabod asked himself. *An accident. A drunken plunge after a night of carousing.* That was the usual explanation. Well, that and suicide— the Hudson River had claimed its share of men with broken dreams.

Or was it murder—a bad debt, perhaps?

Ichabod held his lantern over the body, searching for bruises or cuts. But the light was too erratic, too faint. Clearly the body must be examined. If it *was* murder, the offender was still at large.

The creaking and scraping of rusted metal wheels preceded Green and Witherspoon. As the men finally came into the light, Ichabod was relieved to see that along with the wheelbarrow they had brought a blanket. Already the eyes of the dead man seemed to have burned a place in Ichabod's brain.

The three constables loaded the corpse onto the wheelbarrow. Ichabod made sure to drape the blanket so that the face was covered. Grimly, wordlessly, the men pushed the creaky cart toward the center of the metropolis.

The watchhouse yard was empty, giving it an absurdly peaceful quality. That would shatter at dawn's first light, of course. Throughout the daytime any visitor not used to the ways of New York might mistake the grounds for a madhouse.

But now, in the empty blackness of night, the cart's wheels echoed loudly as Ichabod and his cohorts entered the main watchhouse chamber. Through the bars of the jail cells, the yellow eyes of convicts followed the men's movements.

The high constable was waiting. His features, smothered beneath a thicket of mustache and beard, remained unmoved as he lifted the blanket to examine the body. "Burn it," he said.

"Yes, sir," snapped Constable Green.

Immediately Constable Witherspoon began wheeling the body away.

Ichabod was stunned. Surely the high constable knew better than to destroy evidence.

"Just a moment, if I may," Ichabod blurted out. "We do not yet know the cause of death."

"When you find 'em in the river," the high constable replied slowly, "the cause of death is drowning."

"Possibly so, if there is water in the lungs," Ichabod said. "But by pathology we might determine whether or not he was dead when he went *into* the river."

The high constable stiffened. "Cut him up? Are we heathens? Let him rest in peace—in *one* piece, as according to God and the New York Department of Health!"

Ichabod stifled a protest. It was no use. The high constable was not to be contradicted—by anyone.

A flurry of shouts and scuffles broke the tense quiet. Through the watchhouse entrance, two other constables dragged in another victim. This one was alive but bloody and half senseless.

"What happened to him?" the high constable demanded.

"Nothing, sir," one of the officers replied. "Arrested for burglary."

The two men shoved the victim against the iron bars. He hit with a loud, sickening clang and cried out in pain.

One constable threw open the jail-cell door, then pulled out his leather truncheon. Together the two men bludgeoned their victim until he fell writhing into the cell.

Ichabod averted his eyes.

"Good work," the high constable said.

No, the worst work, Ichabod said to himself. *The work of a society whose growth has exceeded its compassion and logic.*

If the high constable would not listen to his plea personally, Ichabod was determined to seek a public forum. The next morning a semiannual crime-fighting presentation was to occur at the watchhouse. At the invitation of the besieged police department, citizens were to present crime-fighting ideas. The high constable, the burgomaster, the aldermen, and the magistrates would offer a cash contract for the best of the presentations.

Ichabod decided to attend—as a civilian participant, not a constable.

He arrived at the watchhouse shortly after dawn. Through the windows came the deafening clamor of a New York morning: milkmen and chimney sweeps, bakers and bellmen, hot-corn girls whose overflowing baskets sent a sweetly warm aroma into the sweat-choked room.

The presentations were loud and rushed. It seemed every inventor, eccentric, and crank in New York was attending, many having arrived before daybreak. Each idea seemed more ludicrous than the last— most, Ichabod noticed, motivated more by greed than justice.

"And in a few weeks, the plague of pickpockets will be a thing of the past!" announced a shifty-eyed man, shouting to be heard. He held up an odd-looking leather wallet. Onto it had been sewn a metallic gadget resembling a mousetrap. "Give me a dozen constables in gentlemen's dress mixing with the crowds where pickpockets are rife!"

He pocketed the trap. Then, with a flourish, he held aloft a short stick attached at one end to a wooden hand. Slowly he moved the hand toward his own pocket. "A stealthy hand dips into the gentleman's pocket, and—"

Snap! The trap lurched.

With a grin of triumph, the man withdrew the wooden hand. Its fingers had been cut off.

Ichabod winced. The device was ridiculous, barbaric.

"Thank you," the burgomaster said with a polite nod. "We will take your device under consideration, Mr. Vanderbilt. Next?"

Ichabod leaned forward, trying to attract the officials' attention. Surely they'd see him before seeing another of these Gothic monstrosities.

The high constable ignored him. "Mr. Tomkins!"

Mr. Tomkins was even more ragged than the last man. His invention resembled an animal cage.

Ichabod sprang to his feet, unable to restrain himself. "Gentlemen!" he cried out. "In a few months we will be living in the nineteenth century—"

"Wait your turn, Constable Crane," the high constable interrupted.

Ichabod barreled on. "These devices are unworthy of a modern civilization—"

"Quiet!" the burgomaster barked. "Next, I say!"

"Thank you, sir," Tomkins shouted, pulling open the cage door. The floor was solid steel. A writing board dangled by a string on the cage's bars, and a metal clamp hung from the ceiling like a chandelier. "The Tomkins self-locking confessional is cheap—

and it will last for years with just an occasional wipe with a damp cloth!"

Ichabod began writing furiously on a sheet of blank paper.

"When the villain steps on the metal floorplate—" Tomkins continued.

"Arrest this man!" Ichabod shouted.

The high constable glared at him. "Arrest?"

"I accuse him of murder!" Ichabod insisted.

"What are you talking about, you loon?" Tomkins said.

Ichabod gave the man a shove, sending him backward into the cage. Instantly the door slammed shut. The clamp dropped from the ceiling, gripping Tomkins's head.

As the man screamed, the room erupted in bewildered shouting.

Ichabod slapped his sheet on the writing board. "Sign here."

"The . . . release handle!" Tomkins groaned.

"Not until you confess!" Ichabod replied.

Tomkins quickly signed, his face twisted with agony.

Ichabod grabbed the paper, then pulled the release handle. "I have here a confession!" he shouted. "To the murder of a man I fished out of the river last night!"

Tomkins fell limply to the floor. A group of men lumbered to the cage and dragged him away. The platform was in pandemonium.

The high constable stood up, bristling with indignation. "Stand down!"

"I stand *up*, for sense and justice!" Ichabod retorted. "Our jails overflow with men and women convicted on confessions worth no more than this one!"

As the high constable banged his gavel for silence, the burgomaster leaned forward over his dais. "Constable, this is a song we have heard from you more than once, but never before with this discordant accompaniment. I have two courses open to me. First, I can let you cool your heels in the cells until you learn respect for the dignity of my office—"

"I beg your pardon," Ichabod cut in. "I only meant well. Why am I the only one who sees that to *solve* crimes, to *detect* the guilty, we must use our brains? To recognize vital clues, using up-to-date scientific—"

"Which brings me to the second course," the burgomaster continued. "Constable Crane, there is a town upstate, two days' journey to the north in the Hudson Highlands. It is a place called Sleepy Hollow. Have you heard of it?"

"I have not," Ichabod said warily.

"An isolated farming community, mostly Dutch," the burgomaster explained. "Three persons have been murdered there, all within a fortnight—each found with his or her head lopped off."

Ichabod blanched. "Lopped off?"

"Clean as dandelion heads, apparently. Now, these ideas of yours, they have never been put to the test—"

"I have never been allowed to put them to the test!"

"Granted. So you take your experimentations to Sleepy Hollow and deduce—er, *detect*—the murderer. Bring him here to face our good justice. Will you do this?"

The prospect was appalling.

Revolting.

And a golden opportunity.

Ichabod swallowed his doubt. "I shall," he said, "gladly."

The burgomaster smiled. "And remember: it is *you*, Ichabod Crane, who is now put to the test."

2

SLEEPY HOLLOW.

To Ichabod the name conjured up farmers and dirt roads. People of great strength and little literacy. Drafty houses crawling with rodents and spiders.

Most of that he could adjust to, he supposed—except spiders. He detested spiders.

It's only temporary, Ichabod told himself.

His coach was due at dawn. Already the sky was brightening over the gabled roofs across the street. He hadn't slept all night, staring out the window as if he'd never see the city again.

Ichabod bade a silent, temporary farewell to the accumulated detritus of his life: his books and papers, his magnifiers and chemicals, his scribble-coated chalkboards and yellowing anatomy charts.

With a rueful smile, he lifted a birdcage to the window and opened its door. Inside, a pet cardinal cocked its head twice, as if questioning its sudden good fortune.

"Such a day for such a sad farewell," Ichabod said. "But this is good-bye, my sweet."

The cardinal leaped off its perch and flew away. Ichabod watched as its fiery red plumage was consumed in the rays of the rising sun.

Below, a coach pulled up to the bluestone pavement.

They reached the Sleepy Hollow mile marker after two and a half days, and two and a half thousand potholes.

The coach bounced violently. Ichabod angled his head to avoid hitting the knot of bruises that had already formed. He felt compressed, his body rumpled and scarecrowlike, his nerves jangled like frayed piano wire. He hadn't been able to sleep at night for the howling of wolves.

Carefully he checked the contents of his leather satchel. Afternoon sunlight angled in sharply through the western window, glinting off his magnifiers and detection instruments.

The childhood scars on Ichabod's hands stood out in the light, intersecting the lines of his palms. He rarely noticed these scars, rarely wondered about their origin anymore. He preferred solvable mysteries, and this one made his brain fold darkly inward like a frightened sowbug.

There—the road to Sleepy Hollow.

It was long, straight, and well-trodden, the entrance flanked by two massive stone pillars.

The horse slowed to a stop, without entering.

"She'll only go this far," the coachman muttered. "You're on your own from here."

An auspicious start, Ichabod thought. He paid the

coachman and trudged down the long road, loaded down with luggage.

Had he looked up, he would have noticed three odd dark objects on the overhanging elms: dead ravens, hung with twine.

He walked on, his arms throbbing as he approached the center of the village. The setting sun cast a somber stillness over the cluster of small houses and shops. A steepled church stood apart from them, surrounded by a wrought-iron fence.

It was a quiet, unremarkable place.

A bit too quiet, Ichabod thought.

He spotted an elderly woman on the porch of her clapboard house. He tipped his hat, but she backed inside and slammed the door. A man, peering out of a second-story window, suddenly drew his shutters closed.

Looking up, Ichabod spotted men on the rooftops—at least four or five of them—clutching rifles and eyeing the horizon. He passed them, moving out of the town square and onto a rolling field.

In the middle of the field sat a wooden bunkerlike building, topped by a large, clappered bell. Several more townsmen stood around it. They were roughhewn and dressed in farmer's garb. All of them carried rifles, too.

Suddenly Ichabod was distracted by a distant movement at a place where the field met a dense forest. There, as the sun set below the treeline, townspeople lit torches set at regular intervals on wooden posts.

A boy, not more than ten years old, crossed the field to the bunker. He carried a picnic wrapped in a cloth, which he gave to one of the riflemen.

The man smiled gratefully. "Don't worry, son," he said.

It's as if the village is under siege, Ichabod thought. *Can this possibly be a reaction to the murders?*

It seemed, to say the least, extreme.

He set down his baggage and checked a small card. On it, the burgomaster had written the address of Baltus Van Tassel, the man who had sought the city's help.

To reach the Van Tassel manor, Ichabod had to traverse a section of woods and a stream spanned by a covered bridge. The house stood on a hill, overlooking vast rolling grounds. It was large and sturdily built, with a high-ridged but low-sloping roof. Its style, as far as Ichabod could tell, was neither Dutch, French, nor English, but had elements of them all. Across a field stood an old windmill, its weatherbeaten clapboards a great contrast to the manor's opulence.

Lights blazed from the windows of the house; its walls and railings were decorated with jack-o'-lanterns and signs of the harvest. As Ichabod approached, he heard music and laughter. Through the amber-lit windows, spirited couples danced across a grand ballroom. The gloom that gripped the center of town seemed oddly distant.

Ichabod's pulse quickened. His throat was parched. He had been hoping to meet Baltus Van Tassel in a quiet setting. He detested social gatherings. He found them so awkward, so dictated by strange rules of behavior.

He paused, rearranging his rumpled clothing. Then, stiffly, he walked toward the front entrance. As he climbed the steps and passed into the shadow of the front porch, he bumped into a body.

Startled, he jumped aside. He saw that it was two bodies, actually. A middle-aged, prosperous-looking man and a servant girl—very much alive and very much surprised at having been caught in the midst of a furtive kiss.

Nodding quickly, Ichabod pulled the front door open. A blast of sound attacked him as a small orchestra struck up a waltz in the main hall. Smiles surrounded him—intense, insistent, assessing smiles—sizing him up and welcoming him at the same time.

How can they rejoice at a time like this, Ichabod wondered, *when the rest of the town behaves as if preparing for an attack?*

Sweat prickled under his collar as he made his way through the house. When he asked after Baltus Van Tassel, a young woman directed him to the parlor. There guests stood in a thick circle, shoulder to shoulder, intent on a game. In the circle's center, a hale, broad-shouldered man spun a blindfolded young woman.

As he released her, the guests fell silent. She began a wobbly circle around the room, chanting, "The Pickety Witch, the Pickety Witch, who's got a kiss for the Pickety Witch?"

She lurched toward the crowd with open arms, and people jumped aside with gasps of suppressed laughter. The young man barely missed being snared.

Ichabod edged his way around the room, scanning the faces, trying to guess which of the men was Baltus Van Tassel.

"The Pickety Witch, the Pickety Witch, who's got a kiss for the Pickety Witch?"

The embrace knocked Ichabod off balance. She had him. He felt the curious, wary eyes of all the guests.

Please no. No no no no.

Ichabod tried to pull away, but the young woman raised a long, delicate hand to his cheek. Honeysuckle, that was her scent, intoxicating and sweet. Her hair was the color of spun flax, and her simple hand gesture seemed to wipe away days of fatigue.

Across the room, the broad-shouldered young man glared at Ichabod, his face dark with jealousy.

"A kiss! A kiss!" a child cried out.

"She has to guess first!" chimed a well-dressed woman, who gently took the arm of her middle-aged husband.

Ichabod recognized the husband. He was the man on the porch, the one who had been with the servant girl.

"Is it . . . Theodore?" the blindfolded young woman asked.

The crowd roared. A neighborhood joke, clearly.

"Pardon, ma'am," Ichabod squeaked. "I am only a stranger."

The young woman smiled. "Then have a kiss on account."

Before Ichabod could protest, she planted her lips on his cheek and bounced away with an impish smile. As she took off her blindfold, Ichabod's legs almost gave way.

Her eyes arrested him. They were luminous, gimlet-sharp, and yet softly curious. Strong and intelligent, yet full of secrets.

She was exquisite.

"I—um, I—" *Compose yourself, man.* "I am looking for Baltus Van Tassel."

"I am his daughter," the young woman replied, "Katrina Van Tassel."

The broad-shouldered young man appeared behind her. "And who are you, friend? We have not heard your name yet."

"I have not said it. Excuse me—"

The man's arm lashed out. He grabbed Ichabod by the collar. "You need some manners!"

"Brom!" Katrina yelled.

"Come, come!" a deep voice called out. "We want no raised voices."

Brom's grip loosened. Ichabod turned to see a tall man, expensively dressed and powerfully built, with a kind but careworn face. At his side was an elegant lady, sophisticated and attractive.

"It is only to raise the spirits during this dark time that my good wife and I are giving this little party," the man continued.

Brom released Ichabod and backed away.

"Young sir," Baltus Van Tassel said, "you are welcome even if you are selling something."

"Thank you, sir," Ichabod replied. "I am Constable Ichabod Crane, sent to you from New York with authority to investigate murder in Sleepy Hollow."

A murmur swept through the room.

A group of four men reacted with special interest. Ichabod's police-trained eyes lit quickly on them: One was the man from the porch, the two-timer. Near him was a doddering, myopic fellow and a drunken-looking magistrate.

But it was the fourth, a preacher with a doughy,

self-satisfied face, who reacted first: "Well, what use is a constable?"

Baltus's wife, Lady Van Tassel, gave the old man a scolding glance, then quickly turned back to Ichabod. "Sleepy Hollow is grateful to you, Constable Crane. I hope you will honor this house by remaining with us until——"

"Until you've made the arrest!" Brom blurted out.

Laughter—uneasy, sarcastic, frightened—greeted this remark.

So much fear and skepticism, Ichabod thought. *They need me here. They should be relieved, hopeful—yet they scoff. Is the murderer so powerful, so elusive?*

"Come, sir, we'll get you settled," Baltus said.

As he turned toward the door, Ichabod followed. He felt the eyes of Brom Van Brunt on his back until he left the room.

Anatomy. Physiology. Case Histories: Murder.
Ichabod arranged his books on the shelves of his bedroom. It was a comfortable if not luxurious space, with a mahogany desk and an ample fireplace.

Baltus had invited Ichabod to return to the parlor after he had rested and washed up. Then Ichabod could present his case before the prominent men of the town.

But try as Ichabod might to concentrate on his presentation, he could not take his mind off Katrina. Each breath brought in the scent of honeysuckle, each flare of the hearth rekindled the memory of the chandelier's reflection in her hair.

Stop. You saw the eyes of her beloved. You want to solve the murder mystery, not add to the body count.

Ichabod spun at the sound of the door latch.

Sarah, the servant girl and the doctor's secret lover, had entered. Ichabod felt his face flush. She carried a pitcher of water, which she set on a washstand.

"Thank you," Ichabod said. "Please tell Mr. Van Tassel I will be down in a moment."

"I will, sir," Sarah replied. She backed out the door, then stopped before closing it and cried out, "Thank God you are here!"

Ichabod was surprised at the outburst. He suspected—and hoped—that more people felt the same way.

The final strains of music filtered up from below. The party was ending. He would have to go down now.

He poured the water into a bowl. He splashed it over his face and shivered.

As the last guests left, four men remained in the parlor with Baltus and Lady Van Tassel. They sat tensely, waiting for Ichabod, as the servants bustled about, cleaning up.

Magistrate Philipse took a sip of his postprandial cognac. Baltus Van Tassel was famed for the finest liquor in the hamlet, and Philipse could attest to every bottle's quality from personal experience. In times of stress, he drank twice as much and spoke very little. He was silent tonight.

Old Notary Hardenbrook squinted as he adjusted his glasses. Fifty-odd years of handling all the official records in the Sleepy Hollow had rendered him blind as a bat, with a disposition to match. "All the way from New York," he grumbled.

"A waste of time!" Dr. Lancaster agreed, eyeing Sarah as she entered the parlor on her way upstairs. Lancaster was just the other side of fifty years old, happily married for twenty-five of those years and determined to atone for the mistake. His collar felt uncomfortably moist, as it did whenever he was overcome by guilt, which was always.

Reverend Steenwyck reacted to each of the men's words with characteristic disdain. His features were more puffy and righteous as he craned his wattled neck at Baltus. "What can *he* do?" he asked.

"Gentlemen, gentlemen," Baltus said reassuringly, urging them to wait and let the man speak his piece.

As Sarah passed the good doctor, he stretched ever so slightly. His fingers made contact with the hem of her dress, and the trace of a smile crept across his face.

Lady Van Tassel raised an eyebrow and turned away.

Ichabod took a deep breath and opened the parlor door. Sarah was on the other side. She smiled at him briefly, holding the door for him, then closed it as she left.

A firing squad. That was the feeling in the room. Only the Van Tassels seemed happy that Ichabod was there.

"Excellent! Come in!" Baltus called out. Then, leaning toward his wife, he said, "Leave us, my dear."

Lady Van Tassel's smile waned, but she nodded and left.

"We are joined by Dr. Thomas Lancaster," Baltus continued, "and to his left are Clergyman Steenwyck and our able magistrate, Samuel Philipse. And lastly, this fine fellow is James Hardenbrook, our notary."

"And you, sir?" Ichabod asked.

"A simple farmer," Baltus replied to a sudden, chiding quartet of coughs and snickers, ". . . who has prospered." The town looks to me as friend and counsel.

"And landlord and banker," Philipse remarked. "Shall we proceed?"

"Thank you." Ichabod wasted no time getting to the heart of the matter: "So. Three persons murdered. First, Peter Van Garrett and his son, Dirk Van Garrett—both of them strong and capable men, found together, decapitated. A week later the Widow Winship, also decapitated. I will need to ask you many questions. But first let me ask, is anyone suspected?"

Baltus looked at him blankly. "I don't understand you."

"I say, is there any one person suspect in these acts?" Ichabod asked.

The four other men shifted in their seats. None of them looked at Ichabod, but their glances to one another spoke volumes: They had no confidence in the newcomer.

"Constable," Baltus said indulgently, "how much have your superiors explained to you?"

"Only that the three were slain in open ground and their heads found severed from their bodies—"

"The heads were not found severed," Reverend Steenwyck interrupted. "The heads were not found at all."

"The heads are gone?" Ichabod asked, astonished.

"Taken." Hardenbrook leaned forward, his rheumy eyes struggling to focus on Ichabod. "Taken by the Headless Horseman. Taken back to hell."

This was not at all what Ichabod had expected. Nothing in his case studies had prepared him for this.

"P-pardon me," Ichabod stammered. "I—"

"Perhaps you had better sit down," Baltus suggested.

As Ichabod took a seat by the hearth, Baltus pensively lit his pipe. He poured a drink for his guest, then settled back to tell the story of the Headless Horseman.

3

"THE HORSEMAN WAS A HESSIAN MERCENARY," Baltus Van Tassel began, "sent to our shores by German princes to keep Americans under the yoke of England. But unlike his compatriots who came for money, the Horseman came for love of carnage. And he was not like the others."

The four men eyed Ichabod, who leaned forward, trying to ignore them.

"He rode a giant black steed named Daredevil," Baltus continued. "He was infamous for taking the horse hard into battle, chopping off heads at full gallop. His battle-ax was a size and heft that two ordinary men might lift with difficulty. It was honed to the sharpness of a fine razor. And it was only one weapon among an arsenal he kept strapped to his uniform, including a barbed sword. To look upon him made your blood run cold, for he had filed down his teeth to sharp points to add to the ferocity of his appearance."

Baltus bared his teeth in a feeble approximation

that nevertheless chilled Ichabod and drew a chuckle from the men. Smiling wryly, Baltus sipped his cognac and went on. "The butcher would not finally meet his end until the winter of 1779, twenty years ago, not far from here, in our Western Woods.

"He was hiding, preparing for another mission of plunder, but he had underestimated the Revolutionary soldiers. They made up for their threadbare clothes and meager arms with an abundance of grit and cleverness. On that bleak day, they had tracked him to his lair, and they had brought their heaviest artillery.

"A cannon shot ripped through the trees. It missed the Hessian, but the explosion injured Daredevil. The man was deeply attached to his horse, and his already murderous heart turned even more vengeful. However, he was not prepared to face the six Revolutionary soldiers who ambushed him. They were a ragtag lot, dressed in soot-stained, ripped clothing—but they were armed with muskets.

"The Horseman had no choice but to flee. He outran his attackers, pausing for breath in a secluded clearing behind a cluster of trees. There he would mount his own surprise attack."

Here Baltus paused to light a pipe, relishing Ichabod's rapt attention.

"But he was not careful enough," Baltus continued. "From his hiding place came the snap of a branch, so loud that it rang out in the desolate forest like a pistol shot.

" 'There!' arose a cry among the soldiers. They closed in fast from all sides, surrounding him. One rifleman dropped to his knees and took aim. The Horseman reacted quickly. With one arm, he drew his sword. With the other, he grasped a dagger and hurled it. The blade met its mark, in the center of the rifleman's left eye."

Ichabod felt his stomach churn. He set down his drink.

"A second soldier fired," Baltus continued. "The bullet ripped into the Horseman's arm, forcing him to drop the sword. A lesser man would have fallen, but the Hessian's physical strength was equaled only by his blood lust. With his good arm, he clasped his battle-ax and charged the five remaining men.

"The sounds of clanging metal were heard clear across the waters of the Hudson River that wintry day—until a well-thrust sword pierced the Hessian's side and brought him to his knees. Even in his weakened state, he took his attacker's life with a sudden, gruesome swing of his ax.

"As the Horseman struggled to pull out the sword from his own body, the four remaining men overpowered him. The Hessian might have bled to death, but the soldiers would not take any chances. As he struggled to remove the blade, they closed in on him.

"They cut off his head with his own sword. And they placed his body in a shallow grave, throwing the head in after it.

"It is said that Daredevil, limping and wounded, found his way to the gravesite to die by his master's side. To this day, the Western Woods is a haunted place where brave men will not venture, for what was planted in the ground that day was a seed of evil. And so it has been for twenty years."

Baltus Van Tassel took a long draw on his pipe. The fragrant smoke snaked around his head, breaking into wisps that slowly disappeared.

A sudden gust of wind made a low whistling sound in the fireplace.

Ichabod shivered.

Steady, man. This is a local tale about a long bygone incident. Completely irrelevant. We must not be distracted from the topic at hand, the murders.

"But now the Hessian wakes," Baltus said. "He is on the rampage, cutting off heads where he finds them."

Ichabod nearly choked on his drink. "Are you saying—is that what you believe?"

"Seeing is believing," old man Hardenbrook said.

"No one knows why the Hessian has chosen this time to return from the grave," Dr. Lancaster added.

"Satan has called forth one of his own!" Reverend Steenwyck exclaimed.

They do believe this. They actually think a ghost committed these crimes. No wonder no one has been able to bring about justice.

"They tell me you have brought books and trappings of scientific investigation." Now Reverend Steenwyck was standing by the side table, picking up the Van Tassel family Bible. "This is the only book I recommend you study."

He dropped the Bible on the table in front of Ichabod. It landed with a hefty thump.

The Bible was a leather-bound, gilt-edged volume, much finer than any book Ichabod owned. He opened the cover with admiration, examining the gold-leafed edges. On the first blank page, a family tree had been carefully drawn. Ichabod instinctively scanned the list of Van Tassels and ancestors, ranging back several generations.

Confounded distractions. Concentrate. Stay on track.

Ichabod shut the book and looked up. "Reverend Steenwyck . . . gentlemen . . . murder needs no ghost come from the grave. Which of you have laid eyes on this Headless Horseman?"

The men glanced at each other uneasily. None said yes, just as Ichabod had expected.

"Others have," Hardenbrook piped up. "Many others."

"You will see him too if he comes again," Baltus added. "The men of the village are posted to watch for him."

Ichabod smiled indulgently. "We have murders in New York without benefit of ghouls and goblins."

"You are a long way from New York, sir," Baltus said.

"A century at least," Ichabod replied. "The assassin is a man of flesh and blood, and I will discover him."

Reverend Steenwyck's perpetual sneer tightened. "How do you propose to do so?"

"By discovering his reason," Ichabod answered. "It is what we call the motive. This mystery will not resist investigation by a rational man!"

He gestured for emphasis, slashing with his arms and sending his drinking glass flying across the room.

The five men looked at one another, trying not to laugh.

Ichabod glanced sheepishly at the floor. The glass had shattered, and so, he realized, had his credibility.

The sounds of the men's conversation floated through the house and up to the room of Katrina Van Tassel. She could make out the voices, more or less, but not the words. Besides her father's, only one other voice seemed to have a tone of kindness and compassion. Too bad the constable was otherwise such an oaf.

Long after the conversation ended, when the brooding young man was in his room, Katrina prepared for sleep. As always, Lady Van Tassel stopped for a good-night chat. She picked up a brush and slowly, rhythmically, began brushing her stepdaughter's hair.

"Well, I'm disappointed," Katrina said. "Our first visitor from New York—he doesn't know where to put himself, and his feet are all over the place."

Lady Van Tassel nodded. "Yes, not like your Brom."

At a knock on the door, she gave Katrina the hairbrush. "Go on brushing. I got to forty-four strokes."

Lady Van Tassel pulled open the door to reveal Sarah. "That constable, he wants the Bible, mum," the girl said, curtseying meekly.

"Bible?" Lady Van Tassel repeated.

"I'll bring it to him," Katrina volunteered.

Sarah curtseyed again, backing away.

As the servant girl vanished down the hallway, Lady Van Tassel raised a knowing eyebrow to Katrina.

"We'll see if his city talk fits him better than his clothes," Katrina said with a smile.

My first day here has raised even more Obstacles than I anticipated. Enemy Number One, I'm afraid, is the superstitious Nature of these good but benighted Country Folk . . .

Ichabod read his own words for the hundredth time. Finally he set down his pen. He hadn't the

mind to continue, nor to look at the books he had
laid on his desktop.

This would be a challenge, an enormous one; he
would be fighting ignorance as much as crime. If
only his thoughts would not continue to be side-
tracked to . . . to her.

*She is promised. Betrothed. To the—the ape—the over-
grown dirt farmer.*

*Work, Ichabod. That is the one thing which will get you
through.*

As Ichabod picked up his pen once again, he heard
a knock on the door. At last, the servant girl with the
Bible. He'd sent her so long ago, he thought she'd
forgotten.

"Yes, yes, come in!" he shouted over his shoulder.
Perhaps that family tree on the Bible's inner leaf
would reveal something. Something odd had caught
his eye during his brief perusal in the parlor, a familiar surname that he couldn't now recall.

Behind him, the door clicked open. Soft footsteps
trod the wooden floor.

"Thank you," Ichabod called out. "Just leave it on
the reading stand. That will be all." *No. She is a resource. You can learn from her.* "Wait. Tell me about that
big brute who seems to be Miss Katrina's—"

As he spoke, he turned around and came face-to-
face with Katrina Van Tassel.

He shot up out of his chair. His hip knocked
against the desk, which thudded against the wall,
sending papers cascading to the floor. "Forgive me! I
asked Sarah to bring me—"

"So, your clever books have failed you," Katrina
said with an amused smile, "and you turn to the
Bible after all."

Ichabod collected himself. "I see I am talked about downstairs."

"In passing only. We have many things to talk about, even in this backward place."

"I am sorry. Please excuse my manner. I am not used to—"

Speechless. She renders me speechless.

"Female company?" Katrina asked.

"Society," Ichabod shot back.

"How can you avoid society in New York? How I should love the opera and theaters—to go dancing! Is it wonderful?"

Ichabod fought the urge to lie, to make himself sound cultured and urbane. She would see through him; she saw everything. "I have never been."

"But there *is* an art museum? A concert hall?"

"I don't know."

"Then you have nothing to teach me."

The words made Ichabod shrink away with disappointment, but an idea was forming. "Perhaps I have," he said. "Do you believe the Van Garretts and the Widow Winship were murdered by a Headless Horseman?"

"Not everyone here believes it is the Horseman."

At last. A realist. "Good!" Ichabod said.

"Some say it is the Witch of the Western Woods who has made a pact with Lucifer."

Ichabod's shoulders sank. Katrina was one of them, after all, provincial and irrational. "There are no witches or galloping ghosts either. Is everyone in this village in thrall to superstition?"

"Why are you so afraid of magic? Not all magic is black. There are ancient truths in these woods which have been forgotten in your city parks."

"If they are truth, they are not magic; if magic, not truth," Ichabod told her.

"You are foolish. When there is fever in the house, it is well known that willow herb roots and a crow's foot must be boiled in the milk of a pure white goat with special charms uttered over the fire—and the fever abates."

"Next time try the herb without the rest." Ichabod had heard enough. "And now I must ask you to excuse me."

"Gladly. I should not have interrupted our town's savior. Good night." Katrina turned and walked toward the open door. "And as to your first question, that big brute you were asking about has proposed to me."

The statement caught Ichabod off guard. "I—I— I'm happy that—"

Katrina looked back over her shoulder. "He's proposed to me . . . *several times.*"

She paused and smiled, letting the last two words linger. And as she left, she seemed to take all the air in the room with her.

Ichabod had to sit down.

Eyeing the Bible, he took deep, clearing breaths. Work needed to be done. Difficult mental work, involving logic and clear thought. No room for sentimental notions and cryptic feminine innuendoes.

He opened the cover to the family tree and began taking notes:

Katrina Van Tassel—born 1777.
Baltus Van Tassel's first wife (Elizabeth Kierstadt)—
died 1797.

Katrina's mother was only two years dead, he realized. Somehow this did not surprise him. He had seen the sadness behind Katrina's smile, the hint of dark corners within her fire and gaiety, of places into which she would let no one. She must have loved her mother with all her soul.

Of course. A mother's death is a wound that never heals, no matter how tough the scar tissue. One can only protect that scar, hide it from others.

And, if necessary, from the self.

All words, all paths of thought, led to Katrina. He allowed himself to imagine holding her, comforting her, and whispering that he knew. That she needn't say a thing, but *he knew.*

And as he thought of her face, another merged with it—similar in some ways, kind and lovely—opening the wound and letting the darkness out of his own cold, forbidden corner.

His mother's face . . .

No. Not now. Stay at your task. It is finally yielding something.

He picked up his pen again, writing with firm resolution:

> The current Lady Van Tassel—Baltus's *second* wife.
> The name of Baltus's uncle by marriage (the husband of
> his father's sister) is *Van Garrett.*

Van Garrett—two of the murder victims, father and son. Could Van Tassel himself be involved? Did he have a motive of some sort?

Ichabod barely noticed the distant rumbling outside as he resumed work.

* * *

Jonathan Masbath heard the rumbling loud and clear in his bunker outside the center of town. He dropped to a tense crouch and peered through the window. Across the field, the trees formed a pitch-black curtain, lit at intervals by torchlight.

The noise was all too familiar. So was the fog. It grew from the ground, spectral and thick, snuffing the torches one by one.

"Come out, devil," Masbath murmured, sighting along the barrel of his rifle. "Come . . ."

As if in answer, someone came.

He emerged from the mist as if it had spawned him. But he was no wisp, no smoky apparition. He rode a black horse whose flanks glistened in the moonlight like polished gunmetal, whose galloping hooves shook the earth. His cape billowed about solid, wide shoulders—and if he was the devil, he had no horns to mark his identity. He had no head at all.

The Hessian was halfway to the bunker when Masbath fired his first shot. The noise resounded over the thrumming of the hooves. The bullet whizzed by, where the head should have been, but the Horseman kept riding.

Masbath reloaded, his hands shaking and slippery. He aimed as best he could, the Horseman's body growing larger in his sight. This time he made contact. Yet the Hessian only picked up speed. Suddenly the bunker seemed scant protection. Masbath scrambled to his feet and ran out onto the field.

SMACK!

Masbath heard the noise as he ran. He knew what it was—the Horseman's ax. It had demolished the bunker's roof, and it had been meant for him.

Masbath's feet were shod with heavy boots, but he couldn't feel them touch the soil.

The trees. They'll protect me.

The Horseman was behind him now, slowed by the attack on the bunker but gaining fast. Masbath plunged into the pitch-blackness of the forest. Branches whipped his face. Roots clutched at his boots.

The hoofbeats followed him, weaving through the trees.

He has no eyes. How can he—

Masbath heard a sudden whooshing sound.

But he never saw the glint of the ax blade as it passed through his neck.

4

"HIS NAME IS GUNPOWDER," SAID MR. KILLIAN, THE owner of the Sleepy Hollow stable. He smiled fondly as he opened a stall containing a small, droopy horse.

He must be joking.

Ichabod had wanted a quick, strong start this morning. It didn't seem likely. Sleepy Hollow indeed. Everything was sleepy here, including the horses.

He set down his satchel. It was heavy, full of detection equipment. He did not have a great deal of money for rental, but surely it was enough for something sturdy and relatively swift, a horse that could chase after a murderer who might be armed.

Gunpowder looked as if he had been through the entire Revolutionary War, and not necessarily on the winning side.

"A brave name," Ichabod remarked. "But have you got something a little younger? Taller?"

Killian looked at him knowingly. "You mean faster."

"Yes."

"A horse to cut a dash."

"Yes," Ichabod replied eagerly.

"No, I haven't."

"Oh."

"Not at the price."

Spoken like a New Yorker, Ichabod thought with disdain. "Well, I'm sure he'll do very well. Thank you, Mr. Killian."

"Good luck, sir," Killian replied. "If you need any help, call my name."

He turned to a corner of the stable and called to his young son, who was feeding another horse. "Go off for your breakfast, Tom! Kiss your mother once for you and twice for me."

The boy smiled and ran off.

Ichabod envied the man's domestic bliss. For a moment he imagined trading places—giving up his quest for truth, exchanging it for a quiet life shared with a kindred spirit, a person he could love more than himself.

He was about to saddle up the horse when he had a sudden idea. "Mr. Killian, I was thinking, about the old widow—"

"Old widow?"

"Widow Winship."

Killian laughed. "Who told you she was old? She

was comely, widowed young and dead before the
bloom was off her."

CRACK!

A shot sounded from outside the window. A rider
was speeding toward them, waving his musket in the
air.

"It's Van Ripper," Killian muttered. "What on
earth happened?"

"Murder! Murder!" Van Ripper shouted. "The
Horseman has killed again!"

Ichabod had no time for doubts. Gunpowder
would have to do.

Already the streets of Sleepy Hollow were filled
with shouts and whinnying horses and squealing carriage wheels. By the time Ichabod threw on the saddle, he was the last one out of town. He dug his heel
into Gunpowder's side, but the old horse seemed to
be confused and in need of a nap.

Brom Van Brunt galloped ahead of Ichabod on a
black steed, as did a gig driven expertly by Philipse.
They all disappeared into the Western Woods, far
ahead of Ichabod and Gunpowder.

It seemed hours before the old horse made it
across the field. When Ichabod finally came upon the
crowd of villagers, Baltus was shouting instructions:
"Mr. Miller, ride back for the coffin cart. The rest of
you keep a sharp lookout."

A young, dull-looking fellow thrust his head forward, staring intently at Baltus.

"No, not at *me,* Glen," Baltus snapped. "I'm not
going to cut my own head off—look to the woods!"

Ichabod guided Gunpowder toward the circle that
had formed around the body.

Many were turning away. Others stood transfixed,

caught between revulsion and sick fascination. In the center, Dr. Lancaster turned over what remained of the victim.

Clean off at the neck.

Ichabod fought to keep his stomach down. It didn't help to see Brom walking toward him, smirking as if this were an amusement at the county fair. "A fine looking animal, Crane!" he said with a laugh.

Ichabod ignored him. He could not take his eyes off the corpse. As he dismounted, he had to clutch the reins. His legs shook violently.

Utter savagery. As if the victim had been butchered for meat.

Ichabod had known the rotting stink of disease and poverty, seen the mangled victims of gang torture, come face-to-face with the daily ravages of the country's most brutal city—but this was worse.

As Ichabod walked forward, Dr. Lancaster glanced up at him. "The fourth victim: Jonathan Masbath."

The rifleman. A father.

"And . . ." Ichabod swallowed. His throat felt scraped and sanded. ". . . the head?"

"Taken," Magistrate Philipse answered.

"Taken?" Ichabod repeated.

Think. There had to be a reason. Every motive is explainable. One has only to put oneself in the shoes of the murderer to understand what he needs.

Ichabod thought back over the volumes of case studies he'd read, the gruesome murders that seemed so unsolvable.

Out of corner of his eye, Ichabod saw Dr. Lancaster agitatedly grab the magistrate by the arm. Philipse shook him off, fumbling for a flask in his back pocket.

It was a tic of motion in the tumult, but Ichabod thought the behavior odd. They looked worried, not shocked, as if they were guilty, which seemed ludicrous. The murderer must have been tremendously powerful. Neither of these men looked capable of wielding an ax.

Sheer nervousness, Ichabod concluded. No one could be expected to keep his professional cool at a time like this. No one except, perhaps, a seasoned investigator.

Imagine what the murderer needs.

A solution took shape in his mind. "Interesting," Ichabod said, "very interesting."

"What is?" Baltus asked.

"In headless-corpse cases of this sort," Ichabod said, pausing to make sure he had full attention, "the head is removed *to prevent identification of the body!*"

Baltus returned a quizzical look. "But we know this is Jonathan Masbath."

"Exactly!" Ichabod shot back. "So why was the head removed?" He glanced around the crowd. All faces were focused on him expectantly.

"Why?" Baltus asked.

"I don't know."

Philipse took another swig.

Ichabod forced himself to look at the corpse. It was arranged neatly, arms to the side, as if for display. "You have moved the body?" he suddenly exclaimed.

"I did," Dr. Lancaster replied.

Aha. Incorrect protocol, as detailed in the police procedure book. "You must *never* move the body!"

"Why not?" Dr. Lancaster asked.

"Because!"

The force of his own voice surprised Ichabod, and

it seemed to impress the villagers. With new confidence, he began snooping around the murder site.

The crowd moved to accommodate Ichabod as he knelt by a large, deep hoofprint. He unclasped his satchel and pulled out a bowl, a bottle of water, and a bag of gypsum powder. Carefully, efficiently, he mixed the water and powder in the bowl until it had the proper consistency of plaster.

"What is that potion?" Brom asked.

"You are the blacksmith, Brom," Ichabod replied, pouring the plaster into the hoofprint. "Ever shoe a horse with a hoof this large?"

Brom gave a grudging nod. "It's big."

Ichabod left the plaster to set. Then, swinging the satchel over his shoulder, he looked around for more prints.

He found one under a pile of leaves. It pointed toward another, farther away than Ichabod expected. He put his own foot in the first hoofprint, then leaped to the next, and the next, and the next.

To the others, it looked as if he was playing some odd schoolyard game. "The man's a fool," Dr. Lancaster whispered to Philipse.

"He's a fool, and we're damned fools!" Philipse's words were slurred, a notch too loud. "But death will make us all equal!"

"Ssshh!" Dr. Lancaster hissed.

"The stride is gigantic!" Ichabod called out. As he turned back, leaping again from print to print, he explained the strange path. "The attacker rode Masbath down . . . turned his horse . . . came back . . ." —now he was back at the body—"came back to claim the head."

Even Brom was riveted now.

"To sum up," Ichabod continued, his mind racing, "head taken . . . big horse. . . . Did this man have any enemies?"

"Well, someone didn't like him!" Philipse blurted out.

Ichabod turned to Van Ripper. Judging from the slack features of the man, Ichabod surmised that the light of understanding rarely crossed his face at all. "Show me where the neck rested."

With a fearful gulp, Van Ripper pointed to a spot on the ground.

From his satchel, Ichabod took out a bottle that contained a green powder. He sprinkled a thin layer over the area where the neck had fallen.

The powder contained a compound that bubbled on contact with blood. The more blood, the more furious the reaction. Ichabod prepared himself for a near explosion.

The powder bubbled slightly, then fizzled.

Bizarre. This was a beheading, for goodness' sake.

"A chemical reaction," Ichabod explained. "It shows there was just a smear of blood, no more."

Van Ripper shrugged. "I didn't see none."

Look at the neck for clues.

Ichabod swallowed his queasiness. He fished out a set of tapering medical pliers and a pair of glasses fitted with magnifying lenses that could be swiveled into place. He knew the contraption looked outlandish, the lenses sticking out in all directions, but it freed his hands. He would need them.

Holding the pliers, he looked at the neck. The wound was gaping, angry, red. For a moment the world began to swirl. He thought he would faint.

Steady, Crane.

His hand vibrated uncontrollably as he closed the pliers on the wound, pulling at the shreds of flesh. He'd never seen anything quite like this.

Sealed. Sealed tight. As if—

The flesh suddenly moved. Ichabod blanched. The movement was a bug, feeding.

He leaped up, stifling a scream. "Interesting!" he exclaimed.

"What is it?" Baltus asked.

"The wound was cauterized in the very instant," Ichabod replied, "as though the blade itself were red hot. And yet, there is no blistering, no scorched flesh."

"The devil's fire!" Philipse cried out.

The faces of the townspeople were drawn, worried. Ichabod didn't blame them, not a bit.

5

" 'BE SOBER, BE VIGILANT'—AS IT SAITH IN THE BOOK of Peter, chapter five, verse eight—'because your adversary the devil, as a roaring lion, walketh about, seeking whom he may devour . . .' "

Reverend Steenwyck read from a Bible, intoning his words loudly over the open grave of Jonathan Masbath. The preacher's voice seemed hollow and blunted in the frosty stillness of the morning.

Ichabod stood by Baltus and Lady Van Tassel. He bowed his head respectfully, along with all the others, but his eyes were vigilant, observing the crowd.

A boy stood alone near the grave marker. His shoulders were sunken with a sadness far greater than his youth would seem to deserve—Masbath's son.

Near him Katrina was crying openly. Brom stood beside her, staunch and dry-eyed, an arm draped protectively over her shoulder.

Ichabod imagined changing places with him for a moment.

When the reverend finished, the villagers began filing slowly away, mumbling to one another with desperate attempts at consolation. Ichabod walked with the Van Tassels. Thoughts tumbled through his mind—images of Katrina alternating with bafflement over the crime.

Who would seal a wound? How? Why?

An answer existed. He knew it. But it might be beyond the scope of his books and equipment. It would have to involve bold, new techniques.

"Mister Constable, sir!"

Ichabod turned to see Masbath's son. "You are Young Masbath," he said.

"I *was* Young Masbath," the boy answered in a subdued voice, "but now the only one. Masbath at your service, in honor bound to avenge my father."

Ichabod smiled. The boy was courageous. "Well, one-and-only Masbath, I thank you. But your mother will need you more than I."

"My mother is in heaven, sir, and has my father now to care for her. But you have no one to serve you, and I am your man, sir."

"And a brave man, too." Ichabod felt for the boy, but he was young, impetuous, untrained. He would only be a burden to an objective criminal study. "I cannot be the one to look after you. I am sorry for your loss, young Mister Masbath."

As Ichabod turned and moved away, Magistrate Philipse staggered up, pulling his sleeve. "Constable."

"Mr. Philipse?"

Philipse looked around furtively, then spoke in a whisper. "Something you should know: Jonathan Masbath was not the fourth victim but the fifth."

"The fifth?"

"Aye. Five victims in four graves!"

"But who?"

Philipse stiffened, distracted by something. Ichabod turned to follow his glance. Reverend Steenwyck was watching the conversation, his eyes narrowed angrily.

When Ichabod turned back, Philipse was gone, scurrying into the crowd.

Maddening. A village full of grudge-holding, bickering eccentrics.

But Ichabod was intrigued. Five victims in four graves—what did it mean? There was only one way to find out, but he would need help, someone strong of build and stomach.

In the graveyard now, several workers were placing headstones on two fresh graves. Ichabod could see the name *Van Garrett* carved into one of the marble surfaces.

Another newly dug grave lay nearby, marked by a simple wooden cross. The Widow Winship, Ichabod assumed.

Killian was now passing by, having lingered at the gravesite of his friend. A likely candidate, Ichabod thought. "Mr. Killian," he called out, "I will need the help you offered."

Killian gave him an appraising glance, then nodded grimly.

He led Ichabod across the field to his stable. Once inside, Killian stopped moving and looked about, as if sensing something was wrong. He pointed to a large feed bin against a wall.

Ichabod opened it gingerly. Inside, curled up on a bed of grain, was Young Masbath.

A temporary home, Ichabod realized. *Probably one of many to come.*

The sight broke down Ichabod's resolve. The boy was an orphan, like himself. Ichabod could help him, and perhaps he could receive some help in return.

"Find a place in the Van Tassels' servant quarters," Ichabod said to the boy. "Wake me before dawn. I hope you have a strong stomach."

"Thank you, sir!" the young man replied.

The digging was grimy, back-breaking work, not helped by the pitch-darkness of night. Killian's lantern provided too little light; his shovels and spades were too small.

Ichabod dug alongside Killian, his two hired men, and Young Masbath, but it was almost daybreak before they had unearthed the three coffins: Peter Van Garrett's, Dirk Van Garrett's, and the Widow Winship's.

Holding a spade, Killian wrenched the lid of the elder Van Garrett's coffin.

Young Masbath gagged.

The body was flattened out, rotted, and eaten by worms. Its head was missing.

One body only.

Ichabod nodded, and Killian replaced the lid.

The two hired men made quick work of the other two lids, setting them down beside the coffins.

Ichabod gazed into Dirk Van Garrett's coffin. It too contained only one headless corpse. As he moved on, the worker quickly covered the coffin again.

Ichabod held a lantern over the Widow Winship's body.

She, too, is alone. Along with Masbath, that makes four bodies in four graves.

The time and energy had been wasted. Philipse was not to be listened to anymore. He was a drunken madman.

As Ichabod turned away, one of the men began replacing the lid.

Unless . . .

"Wait!" Ichabod said abruptly. He knelt by the coffin. The Widow Winship lay inside, under a shroud. Taking a penknife, he cut through the fabric, just above her abdomen. He tried to discern a swelling. A pregnancy would raise the count to five bodies.

The woman had been stabbed in the stomach area. If she was pregnant, the child would have been killed instantly. But it was impossible to tell just by looking. He'd have to open up the body.

Ichabod leaned closer and readied his knife.

"AAAAAAGHHHH!"

Ichabod's heart nearly snapped out of his chest. Out of the night came a skimble-shanked, thick-waisted, spectral figure in a white nightgown. He lurched toward them wildly, holding a lantern.

"Sacrilege!"

Ichabod immediately recognized the voice, and the profile. It was Steenwyck, his face twisted and deathly in the lantern light.

Ichabod took a deep breath. There was no cause for alarm. This was nothing but a sanctimonious old fool.

"Science!" Ichabod retorted. "Science, Reverend Steenwyck! Someone in Sleepy Hollow is using the Horseman story for his own murderous purpose, and I intend to dig it out!"

Reverend Steenwyck backed away, his face ghostly white.

Ichabod returned to his task. Before dawn, the Van Garretts must be reburied and the widow brought indoors, away from the glare of Steenwyck and his followers.

Dawn had broken, gray and misty, as Ichabod knocked on Dr. Lancaster's door.

The doctor seemed belligerent as he pulled open the door, ready to scold. But his expression gave way to one of mute horror as Killian, Young Masbath, and Ichabod barged by him with a coffin.

They went straight to the medical room.

"This is most irregular, Constable!" Dr. Lancaster bellowed.

"I should hope so, Doctor, but in this case, necessary," Ichabod said as the two men put the coffin down on the floor. "I shall need to operate."

"Operate?" The doctor was apoplectic. "She's dead!"

"When we say 'operate,' we mean, of course—er, I'll need the operating table," Ichabod replied. "Lay her out, please."

Young Masbath recoiled.

"Go on," Ichabod said. "Nothing to be afraid of."

As the two men lifted out the body, Ichabod carefully studied the notes in his ledger, looking for a passage, a clue that might tell him he was on the right track. "There is a common thread between these victims," he murmured.

"And what's that?" Dr. Lancaster demanded.

Ichabod closed the book with a tense sigh. "I don't know."

The body was laid out, dirt covered and stinking. Young Masbath stumbled to a corner, holding his stomach.

First Ichabod examined the neck, then the stab wound. "Once more, the neck wound cauterized. The sword thrust to the stomach, the same. Perhaps it was done by some chemical means. But to what purpose?"

He gingerly placed his hand on the corpse's abdomen, pressing, feeling for what might have been the widow's child.

The doctor bristled. "To what is *your* purpose, is the question."

He suspects what I'm up to. Of course. He's a doctor. He'd be a fool not to know.

Ichabod's hands could feel nothing significant. It was impossible to determine anything by touch alone. He'd have to resort to more precise methods with his own implements. This would be the perfect time to try them out for the first time.

From his satchel he pulled out a handful of metal surgical tools. They were wrapped carefully in a velvet cloth, which he unrolled on a table.

"What manner of instruments are those?" Dr. Lancaster asked.

"Some of my own design," Ichabod answered.

A scalpel. A separator. A clamp.

First the incision, which would need to occur . . . where?

He looked from the table to the body. Killian, Lancaster, and Young Masbath stared at him. Curious. Skeptical. Appalled.

"Step outside," Ichabod said to Young Masbath. "Thank you for your help, Mr. Killian. And if you do not mind, Doctor, my concentration suffers when I am observed."

Young Masbath scampered out the door, followed by the other two men.

Ichabod waited until the door was closed. Then he pulled a large book out of his satchel: *Human Anatomy.*

Opening it to the appropriate page, he studied the drawings, memorized what he could, and picked up his scalpel.

He left the book open for handy reference.

An hour later, Ichabod emerged from the room. He wiped his hands meticulously on a cloth. He wished he could wipe from his mind what he'd just seen.

Dr. Lancaster, Young Masbath, and Killian were no longer alone. Reverend Steenwyck and Magistrate Philipse had joined them, along with a group of townspeople.

A shudder went through the room at the sight of Ichabod's bloodied hands. A notable exception was Philipse, who made a burplike noise and wobbled.

"I am finished," Ichabod said.

"What in God's name have you done to her?" Reverend Steenwyck demanded. "Magistrate Philipse, you are the word of law here. Put him in irons!"

Philipse took a nip from his flask. He glanced at

Ichabod tentatively. "And what did you find out, Constable?"

"That there are not four victims but five," Ichabod replied. "The Widow Winship was with child."

"What of it?" Dr. Lancaster thundered. "She should have been left to make her peace with God, not be cut to bits by the constabulary!"

The words shook Ichabod. He had heard them before, in the police watchhouse from the mouth of a sophisticated city professional—his superior, the high constable. Clearly these feelings cut deep, so to speak.

He scanned the faces in the room, finding expressions of shock, revulsion, condemnation, all directed at him.

He was not making converts.

Carry on, he told himself. *Do not doubt. The widow's soul has made its peace with God. What's here is not the Widow Winship. It is merely a body.*

"The sword was thrust into the womb and no farther," Ichabod announced. "A symbolic murder. We are dealing with a madman."

A whole day and no further clues.

Ichabod watched his and Gunpowder's long shadow play across the trees of the Western Woods. On his way from town to the Van Tassel manor, he was looking for a dropped weapon, a piece of clothing, anything that might bring him closer to a theory.

He would need one, fast.

The morning's events had created a tumult in Sleepy Hollow. Rumors and lies had begun to spread that Ichabod was a fraud, a pervert, a consort of the devil. His residency in New York City seemed to be ample proof of it all.

Had the inspection of the corpse been worth it?

What of the dead child? Why was it important? Who was the father?

The questions lingered as the daylight waned. Among the thick and brooding branches, afternoon was quickly giving way to night. He heard the rushing current of a river and headed for it, hoping he was near the covered bridge that led to the Van Tassel field.

As the bridge's long, wooden shed came into sight, Ichabod smiled with relief. Gunpowder's clopping hoofbeats were loud and rhythmic on the bridge's wooden planks. They echoed throughout the length of the shed, the sound delay making it seem as if another horse was entering.

Soon the echo itself seemed to change rhythms. Ichabod turned around. The hoofbeats stopped. He could see nothing in the blackness behind him. "Who's there?" he called out.

No answer.

It was merely an echo. Your nerves are frayed. That's all.

He began humming. Gunpowder reached the end of the bridge and walked onto solid ground. Behind them, the other hoofbeats continued.

Ichabod swung Gunpowder around to face the bridge. From the black hole of the shed, a horse emerged. Its eyes glinted sharply in the moonlight. It moved slowly toward them, revealing a long neck and high, muscular withers.

The rider came into view. He had high, polished leather boots and a long cloak. Ichabod squinted to see the man's face.

He had none. Above his shoulders was nothing.

Ichabod dug his legs into Gunpowder's side. The horse took off into the forest, fueled by fear to a speed Ichabod had never thought possible.

"Go!" Ichabod cried.

Gunpowder leaped over brambles and boulders. He took the open ground with the agility of a horse half his age, but the hoofbeats behind them were growing louder.

"YEAAGH!"

The cry was unearthly. It seemed to emanate from the trees themselves. Ichabod looked over his shoulder. The rider was rearing back, throwing something.

A large, irregular, round object hurtled toward him—with three openings that gaped wide, spitting flames.

Two eyes and a mouth.

A head.

Ichabod screamed.

The head smashed against his face and he fell. Fire leaped around him, exploding from the brush, igniting the chunks of flesh that tumbled to the ground.

The hoofbeats were coming closer, slowing down. More than one set—a group of horses.

Ichabod tried to see, but the path was swallowed up by the darkness. He scrambled to his feet, nearly stepping on the remains of the burning flesh.

No. Not flesh.

The air had a sweet, familiar smell—pumpkin.

Ichabod glanced around. A chunk of jack-o'-lantern grinned back at him from a clump of grass, mocking his fear. Beside it was a smoldering ball of paper.

The horse and rider loomed before him, the

ludicrously broad shoulders silhouetted in the faint moonlight.

The Headless Horseman reached up to touch the collar of his cape. He grabbed it firmly and pulled.

It was no monster at all.

Ichabod was face-to-face with Brom Van Brunt.

6

"ICHABOD! ICHABOD!"

He is dreaming. That much he knows. He knows the voice that is calling to him, too—female and thrilling.

The ugly thoughts are disappearing. The chase. Brom's prank. The way Brom had sat there in the woods with two friends, Glen and Theodore. All of them laughing, enjoying Ichabod's terror, gaining pleasure at the expense of his sanity.

They had left him there to stamp out the fire. Only Gunpowder had stayed with him. Now he is safe in his room at the Van Tassels'. Katrina is in the house, too, sleeping in her room. Not far away.

In his dream, she is even closer.

She's blindfolded, the way he'd first seen her in the parlor. But she isn't there or in the Van Tassel manor at all. She is standing in a kitchen doorway—his family's kitchen, in the house in which he grew up. She is holding her arms wide.

And he is running toward her, across the yard. His legs brush against the high grass, and he realizes he's not a man anymore. He's a boy again, maybe seven years old, and in his hand are wildflowers that he has picked. For her. Always for her.

When he runs past Katrina into the kitchen, she's laughing. Blundering around, following him with her arms outstretched, the Pickety Witch.

He tries not to laugh himself. Be quiet. That's the game.

But the anticipation is so strong. The fear that she'll catch him. The hope that she'll catch him. He wants to squeal.

"Aaaaah!" she screams, lunging.

She has him now. He shrieks with glee.

Her arms are so long, so full of love and comfort and protection. She kisses him and takes off the blindfold.

She isn't Katrina at all. She's Mother. Young and beautiful and kind, the way he always remembers her. He gives her the wildflowers and she exclaims with delight, pulling one out to put in her hair, her lustrous, perfect hair.

And then, just as he's about to float away on a gust of joy, she flings the flowers away into the hearth fire. They burst into flames, sending tendrils of smoke into the room, but this does not upset him.

She crouches by the fire and beckons Ichabod forward. Her eyes close as she inhales the aroma, sweet and intoxicating. Then, picking up a twig, she begins to draw strange, magical designs in the ashes.

They are enchanting, but they are dangerous. He must not look at them.

A sudden movement distracts Ichabod. The door. It's opening by itself. Slowly.

Magic!

No, it's only the family cat. It slinks in, its fur black and velveteen, its one white paw like a permanent snow-covered boot.

But the cat isn't alone. The doorway fills with another blackness. A shadow, darkly familiar. Ichabod sits up straight and casts a warning glance toward Mother. He must not see what she's doing.

She snaps out of her reverie and stands in front of the hearth. Father walks in. His eyes penetrate. They are locked on Mother.

He knows.

The dream fades out and another fades in . . .

It's nighttime and Ichabod is in his bedroom. The black cat with the white paw is lounging at his side.

They are both watching Mother. She is holding up a paper disk, a new toy. On one side of the disk is a cage. Opposite the cage is a bird. It is pierced by a looped string which can turn it.

She begins to spin the disk. Both items blur for a moment. And then the bird materializes again, inside the cage.

An optical illusion. A wonderful one. Ichabod can't take his eyes off it.

A thunderclap shakes the room. With a loud smack, the window blows open. The cat jumps off the bed and seems frozen in the flash of lightning. The toy falls to the floor.

Ichabod burrows into bed, covering his face. He feels the gentle arms of Mother wrap around him.

Protection.

Warmth.

Love.

* * *

Ichabod bolted up in bed. His neck was sticky, his bedclothes soaked.

The air felt like a slap. The grate was black and emitted no more heat. No fire fed it from below. No one was awake to stoke it.

He could not return to sleep, that much was certain. He was bone cold, and the dream was haunting him. The thought of Mother was painful, too painful. ("She brought it on herself, son. Soon we all must pay for our sins.")

No.

He had to fight the thoughts of Father. They hadn't entered his mind for so long. It had to be that way.

Some questions are better left unanswered. And best forgotten.

He lit a lantern, and the room flickered into visibility. His suitcase. His clothing. His books. His ledger, open on the desk.

My life.

My mission.

Not his.

Never his.

Much work remained. Ichabod was feeling alert. It would be a shame to waste time.

But not here. Another room. To clear his mind— of the dream and of the lingering shock of Brom's prank the previous night, which loomed even larger as the dream faded. Perhaps some food or a cup of warm milk would settle his nerves while he worked.

He stood up and took his ledger. Holding the lantern before him, he tiptoed out of the room and went downstairs.

The kitchen was empty. As he placed the ledger on

the table, he noticed a glow from down the hallway.
Another room was lit. Another soul awake.

Curious, he followed the light to its source, a small
sewing room. Inside, Katrina was reading a book.
The title shimmered in the candlelight—a children's
tale, *The Knights of the Round Table*.

She looked up with a start and closed the book,
covering it with her arms as if afraid to be caught.

"Oh . . . pardon my intrusion," Ichabod said. "I
saw a light."

"It is no intrusion," Katrina replied. "I come here
to read when I am wakeful."

"To read books which you must hide?"

"They were my mother's books. My father
frowned on them then, and he would frown at me
now. He believes that tales of romance caused the
brain fever that killed my mother. She died two years
ago come midwinter."

Brain fever.

Katrina knew the cause of her mother's death. The
cause had a name. Ichabod wondered if she knew
how important that knowledge was, how wretched it
felt *not* to know.

He nodded sadly. "I saw it written in the front of
the Bible."

"The nurse who cared for her during her sickness
is now Lady Van Tassel."

Odd. Ichabod didn't imagine Baltus as the type to
turn to the first pair of sympathetic arms. "There was
something else, too," Ichabod said. "Why did no one
think to mention that the Van Garretts are kith and
kin to the Van Tassels?"

"Why, because there is hardly a household in
Sleepy Hollow that is not connected to every other

by blood or marriage. I have more cousins than fingers or toes to count them on."

"I see."

A cock trumpeted outside. Ichabod glanced out the window at a reluctant silvery dawn. He wondered how many dawns would pass before he would make progress on this case.

"This land was Van Garrett land," Katrina explained, "given to my father when I was in swaddling clothes."

"Given by the dead Van Garrett?"

Katrina nodded. "The Van Garretts were the richest family round these parts even then. When my father brought us to Sleepy Hollow, Van Garrett set him up with an acre, a broken-down cottage, and a dozen of Van Garrett hens. My father prospered and built us a new house. I owe my happiness to him. I remember living poor in the cottage. Should I show you?"

Her experience of poverty only enriched Katrina in Ichabod's eyes. With each sentence, she was drawing him closer.

"Yes," he said. "I would like to see where you were as poor as I am."

Katrina stood. The hem of her skirt lifted off the floor, revealing a slim, well-worn hardbound book.

She picked it up and handed it to Ichabod. "Take this. It is my gift to you."

Ichabod opened the book. His heart sank as he read the title page: *A Compendium of Spells, Charms, and Devices of the Spirit World.*

"But I have no use for—"

"Are you so certain of everything?"

Ichabod did not respond. The book was a gift, a

statement, a bond of sorts. Embarrassed, he leafed through it. He found Katrina's name written on the endpaper and under it the name *Elizabeth Van Tassel*.

"It was your mother's?" he asked.

"Keep it close to your heart. It is sure protection against harm."

Ichabod smiled. "Are you so certain of everything?"

She was probing him with a glance that seemed to see everything. It made him feel uncomfortable and afraid—and deeply, deeply grateful. He placed the book with the others on his desk. Some superstitions, he decided, must be respected.

As Ichabod and Katrina rode across the field, the evaporating dew formed whorls of vapor around their horses' hooves, as if they were traveling on clouds.

The cottage was in ruins, at the edge of a vast farm. Only a hearth and a part of its chimney still stood intact.

Ichabod dismounted and held out his hand for Katrina. She took it and gracefully stepped onto the soft earth. But as he tried to let go, she held on. She was looking into his open palm, at the scars. She took his other hand, too. "These are strange. What are they?"

"I wish I knew," Ichabod replied. "I had them since I can remember."

For the first time in his life, Ichabod did not feel the necessity to shield his scars from view. How strange and wonderful not to be self-conscious or embarrassed. When Katrina looked up at him, her eyes did not judge. They gave. They told him he wasn't alone.

As she turned, stepping over the remains of the

cottage's threshold, Ichabod spotted a flash of bright red on a branch overhead—a cardinal. He smiled. It was as if his pet had followed him. A good omen, he thought—for those who believed in such things.

"I used to play by this hearth," Katrina said. She crouched by the bricks and faced him, twining a flower into her hair. "It was my first drawing school, and my mother was my teacher."

Picking up a twig, she began drawing in the dust. As Ichabod watched, he noticed wildflowers growing through cracks in the flame-blackened floor of the old fireplace. He felt a sudden light-headedness at the sight, at the extraordinary similarity to . . . to what?

The flowers. The drawing. The hair.

"Oh, look!" Katrina exclaimed, wiping the rear wall of the fireplace with her sleeve. A carved figure emerged, a man with a bow and arrow. "I'd forgotten this! See? Carved into the fireback, the archer. This was from long before we lived here."

My dream.

That's what this scene was. But now Katrina was Mother. Doing what Mother had been doing in the kitchen.

Katrina looked at him curiously. "Are you all right?"

Ichabod shook off the image. He managed a nonchalant smile and nodded.

"Oh, look, a cardinal!" Katrina blurted out, pointing up to the tree. "I would love to have a tame one, but I wouldn't have the heart to cage him."

Ichabod unslung his satchel from his shoulder. "Then I have something for you."

He gingerly pulled out something he had brought from New York. It had absolutely no value for his case, but it was the one item he absolutely had had to take with him, if only because he'd have missed it in the event his apartment were ransacked in his absence. He'd had the item since childhood, a paper disk toy on which sat a bird and a cage.

"A cardinal on one side, and an empty cage on the other. And now . . ." He gave the disk a spin. The two figures merged, so that the bird was in the cage.

"You can do magic!" Katrina said with a grin. "Teach me!"

"It is no magic. It is optics." He handed her the toy and demonstrated the spinning technique. "Separate pictures become like one picture in the spinning . . . like the truth that I must spin here."

Katrina held the string.

Ichabod watched the toy bird as it stood at the edge, free, unsuspecting, and oblivious to the prison that seemed so safely far away.

Katrina gave the string a sharp spin. The cage didn't move from its spot, of course, and neither did the bird.

Nonetheless, the trap was all around, the way it is in life. It just depended on how you looked at it.

7

IN THE DARKNESS ICHABOD WATCHED.

Despite the hour, Magistrate Philipse's house was lit. He had company tonight—Reverend Steenwyck, Dr. Lancaster, and Notary Hardenbrook. But this was no friendly gathering. The three men gestured and shouted, badgering Philipse as he packed a suitcase.

He's leaving. Fleeing.

Philipse had been the only one remotely helpful. He had known about the Widow Winship's baby. He undoubtedly knew more. Ichabod could not afford to lose him.

In his hiding place across the lawn, Ichabod quietly mounted Gunpowder. He would have to intercept the magistrate, perhaps on the road outside of town, away from the meddlesome trio. Turning the horse around, he eased it onto the road, gradually spurring it harder until it was galloping away.

Farther along, Ichabod eased Gunpowder into a thicket of trees, where they both would wait.

It seemed hours before the magistrate's horse announced its approach, snorting loudly, protesting the weight of the packs slung over its back. Ichabod and Gunpowder were stone-silent until the horse was almost upon them. Then they pounced. Blocking the road, Ichabod grabbed the horse's bridle.

The old man nearly fell off. "What are you doing? Let go!"

"What are you running from, Magistrate Philipse?" Ichabod demanded.

"Damn you, Crane!"

"Shh. You'll raise the village." Ichabod leaned in close. "You had a mind to help me."

Philipse glanced over his shoulder and lowered his voice to an agitated hiss. "Yes, and I put myself in mortal dread of—"

"Of what?"

"Powers against which there is no defense!"

"How did you know the widow was expecting a child?"

"She told me."

"Then I deduce you are the father."

"I hope your deductions serve you better in your contest against the Hessian," Philipse snapped. "I am not the father."

"Did she tell you the name of the child's father?"

"Yes . . . she did."

The distant bleating of sheep distracted Ichabod, but he ignored the sound. Philipse was finally cracking. "She came to me for advice," the old man said, "as the town magistrate . . . to protect the rights of her child. I was bound by my oath of office to keep the secret."

"Do you believe the father killed her?"

Philipse glared at him. "The Horseman killed her! You damn fool, do you think the Horseman stops to dally with our women?"

"The Horseman?" Ichabod felt his blood rise. "How often do I have to tell you there is no Horseman! There never was a Horseman. And there never will be a Horseman!"

The old magistrate shied away, but Ichabod reached out to grab him. His hands closed around an amulet that hung from Philipse's neck—an iron key. "Let go!" Philipse protested. "It is my talisman that protects me from the Horseman!"

"You, a magistrate, and your head full of such nonsense! Now tell me the name of—"

The sheep were upon them, streaming across the road, without a shepherd in sight. The ground began to rumble violently as if the sheep were the weight of rhinoceroses. Gunpowder bucked and brayed. Philipse's horse rose onto its hind legs. Above them, a flock of birds rose like a black cloud. A wind began to shriek.

Ichabod looked toward the forest. The trees were bending, giving way to a deepening blackness.

Brom, Ichabod thought. But Brom's horse hadn't sounded like cannon fire, and Brom's approach hadn't caused nature itself to flee in terror.

"Oh my," Philipse said, his voice a plaintive moan. "Oh my oh my oh my . . ."

As he frantically spurred his horse on, the woods exploded.

Out of the darkness emerged a monstrous horse, its trunk as thick as a tar barrel, leaping over brambles as if in flight—racing directly toward Ichabod.

On the horse sat a man without a head.

Ichabod reached for his holster, his fingers rattling. A blast of wind sent him tumbling. He crawled away, afraid for his life, but the horse was already past him and gaining on Philipse.

The Horseman unsheathed his sword. It glinted, impossibly bright as he raised it over his head.

The magistrate turned. Shaking, he faced the Headless Horseman and lifted the talisman.

"PHILIPSE!" Ichabod shouted.

The whoosh of the sword was deep and steady. The talisman flew away, toward Ichabod.

Another object, round and heavy, jettisoned away from Philipse in the opposite direction. It hit the ground with a dull thud, moments after the rest of Philipse's body collapsed.

Ichabod scrabbled to his feet, again reaching for his pistol. The Horseman was circling him now. The black horse let out a ghastly scream as Ichabod fumbled with the weapon.

Shoot. SHOOT!

Too slow. The horse was upon him. Ichabod smelled its fetid breath.

But the Headless Horseman galloped right by, circling back to Philipse and lowering his sword to the ground.

With a rude thrust, the Hessian raised the sword high, like a cavalry officer spurring on his charges. At the tip of the blade was the severed head of Magistrate Philipse.

Ichabod watched the Horseman vanish into the Western Woods.

Then he fainted.

Ichabod awoke to a tapping on the door. "Constable Crane?" a voice called.

He bolted up out of bed.

No! Go away! I haven't done anything.

The outlines of his room came into focus—the bookshelves, the grate, the desk. He was in the Van Tassel house, safe again. No longer on the Sleepy Hollow road. No longer facing—

Stop.

It was a dream. A horrible nightmare.

His body was coiled, his right fist clenched so tightly that it ached. He tried to release the images, to relax himself. He opened his hand. Inside it was a small, iron key.

At that moment the door opened. Baltus entered, followed by Katrina and Young Masbath. Their faces were taut with concern.

"It was a Headless Horseman!" Ichabod cried out.

"You must not excite yourself," Baltus said soothingly.

"But it was a Headless Horseman!" Ichabod repeated.

"Of course it was," Baltus replied.

He's humoring me. He thinks I've lost my mind.

"No, you must believe me—it was a Horseman! A dead one. Headless!"

Baltus nodded. "I know, I know—"

"You *don't* know, because you weren't there! But it's all true!"

"Of course it is," Baltus said. "I told you. *Everyone* told you!"

Philipse's head on the sword, skewered. And just moments before, he had been speaking to me. Afraid. Knowing he was in danger.

And I—

I—

"I SAW HIM!"

With that, Ichabod fell to the bed in a swoon.

Young Masbath glanced hopelessly at Katrina. "I suppose it's back to the city, then."

Milkweed seedlings. Millions of them. Filling the air, swirling like a snowstorm in summer.

In the dream, he is far from the Van Tassel house, far from the awful events that brought him there. He is home again, in the woods behind the house, with Mother.

She opens the milkweed pod and blows. The seedlings burst out. So many. They couldn't all have come from such a small place. It must be magic!

He is giggling. The sound is high-pitched, like the pealing of a small bell. Mother hands him a pod and shows him how to open it. He does, and he blows. But as the seedlings fly away wildly over the field, Mother is gone.

There, among the trees! She is running away, playing hide-and-seek. He chases after her, but she is bigger than he, and faster. He loses her. He is suddenly alone and afraid.

No. She's in a small glade, lit with sunlight. She would never lose him. Never.

As he runs closer, he sees that she is inside a circle of mushrooms, orange and white and blue, like colorful little dining tables at a café for salamanders. She is turning, her face to the sky, and then she stoops to pick a mushroom. As she takes a bite, a small piece falls to the ground.

She looks so happy. Ichabod races to the dropped mushroom and gulps it down. Now Mother has noticed him. She takes his hands and spins him around, dancing, laughing.

The trees are a soft blur of green, bobbing up and down, speeding up . . . darkening . . . sharpening. . . .

Soon they are no longer trees. They are human— headless figures, dozens of them. Dressed in black.

Ichabod falls. He is weak, dizzy, frightened. As he looks up, his vision clears. The figures have come together. They are only one man.

He is not headless. He is Father.

Mother hasn't noticed him yet. She is still dancing. Her hair flows; her tightly wrapped clothing now spins loose and free.

Father's eyes are fixed on her. They are glowing like hot coals. His face is twisted with rage.

He steps forward.

And Ichabod closes his eyes . . .

When he opens them, it is nighttime. He is in his house, standing outside the kitchen door. The door is closed, but Ichabod looks through a crack in the paneling.

Mother is seated, looking at the floor sadly. Father is pacing, yelling. He's waving his Bible, quoting from it by memory. Mother has sinned. Dancing is the devil's work. He grabs her by the shoulder, pushing her to her knees.

Now he is reading aloud from the Bible. The book is familiar—the leather cover, the gilt-edged binding is an exact match to the Van Tassel family Bible!

Father is making Mother repeat, forcing her to pray with him, to condemn herself. Ichabod wants to cry out, to burst into the room, but he can't. He can't face . . . him.

He backs away. He turns and runs all the way up to his room. To safe shelter.

BOOOOOM!

At the sound of thunder, Ichabod dives into bed. The driving rain blows open his window. He runs to close it, but he stops, drawn by what he sees outside.

A coach waits in front of the house. A man is dragging Mother toward it. Two other men stand watching, their faces hidden by hat brims. As she struggles, she throws a glance toward Ichabod's room. She is pleading. Her face is terrified, beseeching.

The two men follow her glance, and Ichabod can see their faces. One of them has the cruelest face he has ever seen.

The other is Father.

Ichabod reaches out, through the window, but the other man forces Mother into the coach. Then, at Father's command, the coach moves away.

Run after her! Ichabod tells himself. *Save her!*

But once again, he can't move. Not while Father is standing there.

Lightning flashes again. It bathes Father in harsh blue light. His face is like granite.

Ichabod cannot feel, cannot breathe. He shrinks back into his room, followed by the bright orange eyes of the black cat.

8

BALTUS VAN TASSEL WAS HUNCHED DISCONSOLATELY over the drawing-room table. He had had enough.

He might have expected as much from the New York City police. They patrolled the largest, most resourceful city in the new nation, and yet they cared little for upstate villages.

He had called Reverend Steenwyck, Dr. Lancaster, and Notary Hardenbrook to a strategy meeting. Lady Van Tassel and Katrina hovered nearby, listening, but no one had much to say in the wake of Magistrate Philipse's gruesome death.

"This time I'll go to New York myself," Baltus declared, "and I won't be fobbed off with an amateur deductor."

"Detector," Hardenbrook contradicted him.

"Deductive," Steenwyck spoke up.

"No," Lancaster said, trying to summon another word. "No . . ."

"An amateur sleuth!" Baltus said with disgust. "This time it's a magistrate that's dead."

Ichabod heard the conversation through the drawing-room door, but it didn't faze him a bit. He had awakened with fresh ideas. He was no longer afraid.

Shoving the door open, he strode confidently into the room. "Gentlemen! I need able men to go with me into the Western Woods. Who will be the first to volunteer?"

"You?" Baltus looked flabbergasted. "We thought you'd shot your bolt."

"A setback, merely," Ichabod replied. "And yet a step forward, too. We now know who has done these terrible—"

"*You* know," Steenwyck interrupted. "We *already* knew."

"Quite so!" Ichabod said. "And now it seems fate has chosen me to make my name in a case without parallel in the annals of crime—in short, to pit myself against a murdering ghost."

"No!" Katrina cried out. "Ichabod . . . Constable—"

"Do you intend to arrest him?" Lady Van Tassel asked with a playful smile. "Or impound his horse?"

"Neither," Ichabod answered. "I intend to put an end to the killing, to discover the cause and remove it. Who's with me?"

The silence was unanimous.

Only Young Masbath accompanied Ichabod on his journey into the Western Woods. Despite the early hour, the forest was dark, its gnarled trees looking hunched and cowardly.

The horses trudged along gamely, bearing not only their riders but sacks of equipment, including shovels and Ichabod's satchel.

"The Van Garretts, the Widow Winship," Ichabod thought aloud, "your father, Jonathan Masbath, and now Philipse. *Something* must connect them. Can you think what it is?"

Young Masbath shook his head. "We had no dealings with the magistrate that I know of."

"And the widow? Your father knew her?"

"Everyone knew Widow Winship."

Ichabod raised an eyebrow. "In a manner of speaking, I trust."

"She would bring old Mr. Van Garrett a basket of eggs many a day."

"Did your father have dealings with the Van Garretts?"

Young Masbath seemed startled by the question. "He worked for them. We lived in the coach house."

Something was on the boy's mind. Ichabod looked at him quizzically.

"It's nothing." Young Masbath shook his head. "There were many servants, all dismissed now, of course. But there was something happened one night, a week before the murder. An argument upstairs between father and son, and my father was later sent for by Mr. Van Garrett."

"An argument between father and son," Ichabod murmured to himself. "After which, the elder Van Garrett summoned his servant, Masbath."

Young Masbath halted his horse. "Listen."

"I hear nothing," Ichabod replied.

"Nor I. No birds, no crickets—it's all gone so quiet."

Eerie.

"You're right!" Ichabod cried out.

He spurred Gunpowder into a gallop. Young Masbath was right behind him.

On a hilltop that overlooked the woods, Ichabod and Young Masbath rested.

The Horseman had not come. They'd seen no sign of him at all. Perhaps they'd been hearing things. Perhaps their frayed nerves had played tricks on their brains.

Just below them, smoke twined upward from within a rock outcropping. Moving closer, Ichabod saw a cave. A door had been crudely fitted to an entranceway. The smoke came from a chimney. Perhaps the dweller would know something about the Horseman.

Ichabod and his young helper dismounted. They made their way to the entrance and knocked at the door.

No answer.

Ichabod pushed open the door. Warily they stepped inside. The cave was dim and reeked of strange smells Ichabod couldn't identify. Animal skins and skeletons hung from the wall.

In the midst sat an old woman. Her back was to Ichabod, her body still, her gray hair limp and lifeless.

"The Witch of the Western Woods." Katrina's words came back to Ichabod. They were silly, of course. This was an old hermit, no more, a poor woman with some frightening habits.

Young Masbath was pale. Ichabod tried to comfort him with a glance, but he felt as scared as the boy looked.

"Pardon my intrusion," Ichabod said, edging forward.

The woman did not move as she answered him. "You are from the Hollow?"

"In a way, yes. I, um . . ." Now he could see a table full of scooped-out gourds filled with leaves, acorns, and dead insects. Knives and scissors were strewn among a helter-skelter array of yellowed bones.

Ichabod's stomach lurched.

"I should like to say—" he stammered, "um, I make no assumptions about your occupation nor your ways, witch—*which*—which are nothing to me."

Silence.

"Um . . . whatever you are," Ichabod stumbled on. "Each to his own! Um . . ."

The old crone moved. Her arm reached up to the table, and she opened her fist. A dead bird spilled out—a cardinal.

Ichabod stepped back in horror.

Young Masbath stood beside him. "Do you know of the Horseman, ma'am . . . the Hessian?"

The crone calmly drew a finger across her neck.

Young Masbath gulped. "That'll be him, miss."

Ichabod's eyes fixed on the woman's neck. Around it was a cord, threaded through a strange carved stone, a bauble of some sort.

Rising, the old woman pointed to Ichabod. "You, follow with me." Then she leveled her gaze at Young Masbath. "Go out, child. Keep away. No matter what you hear, keep away."

She took a candle and walked deeper into the cave, down an incline. Ichabod followed her into another room, low and cramped, bestrewn with straw and an odd assortment of jars and bowls. Two metal cuffs hung on chains bolted to the opposite wall. "Um . . . what might he hear that he must keep away from?"

"Sit there." The old woman pointed to a crooked stool, and Ichabod sat.

Turning her back to him, the crone knelt by the wall. She slid her wrists into the cuffs and pulled them taut, testing them. Then she slid her wrists out.

"He rides," she said, "to the Hollow and back. I hear him. I smell the blood on him."

Bizarre.

Dangerous.

Ichabod inched forward. "Do—do you? Well. I'm here to find him and . . . er, make him stop."

"You want to see into the netherworld. I can show you."

The old crone began gathering straw into a pile on the floor. On top of it she placed the gourd bowls along with grass and a strange powder.

"What—what are you doing?" Ichabod asked.

The crone lifted a jar and shook it hard. Holding it upside down, she pulled off the lid. A baby bat emerged, dazed and fragile. The crone grabbed it with one hand. With the other, she took a knife and sliced off its head.

Ichabod was overcome with nausea. As the woman poured the bat's blood over the straw, he prepared to bolt.

"Do not move or speak!" the old lady commanded. "When the other comes, I will hold him."

Ichabod froze as the crone ignited the straw with her candle. "The *other?*"

"Silence!" Closing her eyes, the woman inhaled the smoke deeply. "He comes now."

A wind picked up within the cave, seeming to arise from the fire itself. It drew air through a hole in the wall, whistling, shrieking.

The crone slumped forward, and her face hit the floor.

Ichabod stood up. "Excuse me? Ma'am?"

No motion.

The wind was a gale now. The candles flickered and then blew out.

"Do you hear me?" Ichabod asked.

Suddenly the old woman leaped up—although *woman* no longer seemed apt. Her hunched frame was now massive and hairy, her face that of a slavering beast out of whose eyes snakes slithered: The Other.

It sprang toward Ichabod. He hurtled backward and crashed into a table, which fell to the floor in a shower of bones.

But the creature suddenly jerked backward. The chained cuffs were not giving an inch.

"AAAAIIIIIIIIII!"

The shriek penetrated like a needle. Ichabod scrambled to his feet. He backpedaled until he hit the stone wall.

"You seek the warrior bathed in blood, the Headless Horseman!" The creature clawed the floor, gouging the rock. Its voice was hollow and fierce. "Follow the Indian trail to where the sun dies. Follow to the Tree of the Dead."

With a ferocious jerk, the creature yanked at the chain. The bolt moved from the stone a fraction of an inch. The wall was breaking. "Climb down to the Horseman's resting place. Do you hear?"

Ichabod nodded. He looked toward the door.

CRRRAACK!

The bolt shot out from the wall in an explosion of dust. The creature, free of the restraints, lunged forward, roaring.

Ichabod ran through the archway, toward freedom. But it was too late. The claws grabbed him from behind, around the neck.

Ichabod's cry was muffled by the stone cave. His hands and feet slipped on the slick floor as he struggled against the tight grip.

Then, suddenly, the claws loosened. They fell lifelessly on his shoulders, and Ichabod saw that they were no longer claws. They were the dry, wrinkled hands of the old crone. She had returned from the netherworld, or wherever she'd been. She was semiconscious, groggy and limp.

Ichabod pulled himself out from under her and ran.

Young Masbath sat outside the cave, oblivious.

"We are leaving," Ichabod announced, sprinting away.

"What happened?" Young Masbath asked.

"We are leaving *now!*"

The young man needed no further urging. He and Ichabod mounted their horses and sped off.

9

"HOW WILL WE RECOGNIZE THE TREE OF THE DEAD?" Young Masbath asked.

"Without much difficulty, I rather fear," Ichabod replied.

They were deep in the woods, following a wide, well-beaten path that could only have been the Indian trail. Young Masbath had listened raptly to the tale of Ichabod's encounter with the crone. Rather than deterring the boy, it had only strengthened his resolve.

Ichabod thought for a moment, recalling the next instructions. " 'Climb down to the Horseman's resting place,' she said."

"His camp?" Young Masbath asked.

"His grave."

Both riders fell abruptly silent at a noise, a snapping sound. It was soft, not far behind them.

"Quicken pace," Ichabod whispered.

They rode faster along the trail, picking up speed as they crested a hilltop.

Suddenly Ichabod pulled Gunpowder to a stop and leaped off. "Ride on," he commanded, handing the bridle to Young Masbath.

The boy nodded uncertainly but obeyed.

Ichabod unholstered his pistol. Quietly he walked back up the trail, the way they'd come. He crouched low, listening.

Among the chirping of birds and the screeching of chipmunks was an unmistakable snort—a horse dead ahead.

Ichabod crept forward, then stopped. Ahead of him, almost hidden by the underbrush, was a figure in a gray hooded cloak on horseback, moving slowly.

Raising his pistol, Ichabod tried to line up the figure in its sight. His hand vibrated. His breaths were swift and shallow.

"Halt and turn!" he shouted. "I have a pistol aimed!"

The horse stopped as the figure turned and dropped its hood—Katrina.

"It is me!" the young woman cried out.

Ichabod quickly lowered the gun. "Katrina . . . I might have killed you. Why have you come?"

"Because no one else would go with you."

The words lifted Ichabod, like wind beneath a faltering kite. She was risking her life, disobeying her father to be with him on a mission of hopelessness and peril.

He moved toward her, reaching upward. "I am now twice the man. It is your white magic."

Katrina took his hand. Slowly she leaned at the waist, bringing her exquisite face closer to Ichabod. Closing his eyes, he prepared to meet her lips with his.

"Pardon my intrusion."

Ichabod spun around at the sound of Young Masbath's voice.

The boy's face was red. "I think you'd better come look at this."

Ichabod took a deep breath. He glanced at Katrina, whose radiant face still held a promise he longed to redeem.

They followed Young Masbath into the woods, where the men's horses were tethered. Soon all three were on horseback, trotting down the Indian path. At a clearing, they stopped. No vegetation grew here. A fog seeped up from the barren ground, nearly obscuring the monstrous shape in its center.

It was a tree, misshapen and grotesquely overgrown. It stood on massive gnarled roots that jutted outward like the arms of a giant reptile. Its rotting base was the size of a small hut, and it rose at a sharp angle as if bent in agony, its canopy dense with branches that tapered to leafless spindles.

"The Tree of the Dead," Young Masbath said.

Katrina nodded. "It does announce itself."

Ichabod dismounted and began walking closer. The others followed.

At the center of the tree was a vertical gash where the trunk had been torn asunder as if by lightning. The wound must have been old because the bark had healed over it, forming a kind of scar.

No, not a scar, Ichabod realized. It was fresh, moist. *More like a scab.*

He grabbed a jagged edge of bark and pulled it free. Where the bark had been severed, a globule of sap formed. It began to drip, thick, dark, and red.

Ichabod touched the sap and then sniffed his finger. "Blood."

Katrina blanched. "The tree *bleeds?* How can it be?"

Ichabod went to his saddlebag and took out an ax.

"What is it?" Young Masbath asked.

"Stay here," Ichabod replied.

Turning the ax flat-side out, he struck the trunk. The sound echoed within the tree. It was hollow.

He rotated the ax until the blade pointed to the tree, and he began to chop. With each thrust, the liquid oozed out stronger, festering and flowing. The deep redness was mixing now with another fluid, thicker and greenish white.

Ichabod struck hard, using both hands.

"What are you doing?" Katrina asked.

"Just keep where you are!" Ichabod demanded.

Katrina and Young Masbath moved closer. A jagged flap of bark hung from the tree now, revealing something deep inside. Ichabod dropped the ax and began to pull on the flap, but it held firm.

He leaned back, yanking hard, putting all his weight into it until the bark finally tore loose. An object now jutted from within the exposed trunk, pasty and round and white and entangled by roots.

As Ichabod moved closer to examine the object, he felt a deathly chill. It was a head soaked in blood. Its eyes were wide, its mouth open, frozen in an expression of unspeakable fright.

He had seen the expression before, last night at the end of the Headless Horseman's sword.

Philipse.

Ichabod staggered backward, his hand to his mouth. Behind him, Katrina stifled a scream. Forcing himself to look closely, he realized that below the head were several others—four to be exact, and all were decayed and mangled. At the top was the head of Jonathan Masbath.

"My God . . ." Katrina murmured. She drew Young Masbath's face into her shoulder, turning his eyes away from the sight.

The Horseman arises from here. This is his home.

"He—he tries to take the heads back with him," Ichabod said. "They will not pass—"

"We must leave this place," Katrina said.

"This is a gateway," Ichabod continued, "between two worlds."

According to the legend, he was buried near here.

Ichabod circled the tree, examining the ground, looking for . . .

There. Lying on the ground. The Horseman's sword. His grave marker. It was rusted, entangled with twenty years' growth of roots.

Ichabod knelt and touched the ground. "Climb down to the Horseman's resting place," he commanded. "Bring the shovel."

Gazing up, he saw Young Masbath clutching Katrina, his face buried.

You insensitive fool, he has seen his father in there.

"Forgive me," Ichabod said. "I—"

Young Masbath broke away from Katrina's embrace. He stood tall, wiping tears from his face. "Yes, sir. The shovel. *Two* shovels, and the rifle, I suggest."

Bravely he turned toward the saddlebags.

Ichabod exchanged a glance with Katrina. She was afraid. So was he. But if the boy could stand it, they could, too. The Horseman had to be stopped.

"I'll help dig," Katrina said.

Ichabod and Young Masbath unloaded two shovels and a rifle. "You stand guard," Ichabod commanded.

They walked to the grave. Young Masbath crouched, the rifle at his knees. Dusk was settling as Katrina and Ichabod began digging. Overhead, the squeaking of bats punctuated the silence.

"This ground has been disturbed," Katrina remarked. "The soil is loose."

They struck a solid object, wrapped in burlap. Young Masbath left his post and came closer. The burlap was decayed and worm-eaten. As Ichabod pulled it loose, clods of dirt fell away.

"Look!" Ichabod exclaimed.

Beneath the cloth was a uniform—tattered, moldy, and Hessian. It was like those of the mercenaries Ichabod vaguely remembered from his youth, the marauders who had helped the English during the Revolution.

Within the uniform was the broad, sturdy skeleton

of a man with long legs and arms, a deep chest, broad shoulders, but no head.

"The skull is gone," Katrina said. "What does it mean?"

Ichabod leaped to his feet. "It means, my dear Miss Van Tassel, it means—yes! What exactly *does* it mean? It means, unless I am much mistaken, it definitely means something! What that something is, only time will tell! But I sense that we are very close to the answer here, if only we had one more clue—"

"Ichabod!" Katrina screamed.

Under his feet, Ichabod felt motion. The roots of the tree were alive, undulating like the tendrils of a subterranean beast. He jumped aside, watching in horror as the roots writhed around the frame of the skeleton, pulling it into the soil.

From behind him came a noise, a sucking sound. He spun around. The gash in the tree was swelling, pulling itself inward as if it had turned to liquid.

The severed heads disappeared, drawn into the seething mass. As the gash closed, it began to bubble.

Go. NOW!

Ichabod turned and bounded over the grave. He hastened Young Masbath and Katrina onward.

The horses were chafing, bucking, their eyes wide with fright. The ground began to rumble low and deep, like an earthquake.

There was no time to mount. Ichabod, Katrina, and Young Masbath ran for the trees for cover. Hiding, they turned back to look.

With a loud crack, the wound burst open. A shower of cinders spat outward. And in the midst of the trunk, a light formed.

It quickly grew brighter, until Ichabod had to

shield his eyes, but not before he saw two shapes take form within—Daredevil and the Headless Horseman.

Then, with a thundering boom that seemed to well up from the earth, the light exploded and the beast galloped across the clearing toward the Indian path, its hoofs creating sparks as they struck the soil.

In a moment, horse and rider were gone.

"Did you see that?" Ichabod said, gaping.

Don't just stand there, man. Follow him!

Shaking off his stupor, Ichabod sprang toward Gunpowder. "Take Katrina home!" he shouted over his shoulder.

"Constable, no!" Young Masbath pleaded.

But Ichabod was already on the old horse, giving it a swift, hard kick. Monster or not, the Horseman was not going to get away.

10

BLASTED KILLIAN. BLASTED HORSE. IF ONLY I COULD GO faster!

In the waning light, Daredevil's hoofprints were still visible, but just barely. The Horseman was out of sight.

Ichabod followed the prints down an incline. The path was familiar here. Ahead of them was a hill. At the top, firelight danced angrily in a clearing, silhouetting the surrounding trees. As they climbed the hill, Ichabod slowed Gunpowder. He could see the source of the inferno now: the entrance of the crone's cave.

Gunpowder shied, rearing up on his hind legs. Ichabod struggled to keep the frightened horse under control. Finally he jumped off and made his way on foot.

The flames shot out from the cave like a giant
blowtorch, sending waves of black smoke toward
him. Coughing, Ichabod plunged through, pushing
the smoke away, trying to see.

The ground was rocky here, invisible through the
blanket of smoke. His foot slipped and he fell hard,
sliding on a hard, sloping boulder.

He landed on his hands. When he lifted them, they
were deep red. The rock was coated with blood. Beside him lay an inert figure—a body, clothed in rags.

Ichabod gasped, backing away. It unmistakably
was the crone, despite her lack of a head. The skin of
her severed neck was shredded, and it still bled.
Blood was everywhere—gathered in pools by the
cave entrance, slickening the surrounding rocks, wet-
ting the scattered leaves.

Ichabod fought back his disgust and tried to think
clearly. Something was missing. Something else.

The stone amulet. It's gone, too.

A horse's whinny pierced the sound of the raging
fire. It wasn't Gunpowder; the sound was too loud,
too powerful.

Daredevil?

Ichabod squinted, trying to see through the
smoke, but it was impossible. He could only listen as
the hoofbeats grew dim, galloping away.

Deeper into the forest, Brom Van Brunt pulled his
horse to a halt. As he held up his hand, his friends
Theodore and Glen stopped their horses, too. Brom
took the musket from around his neck and clutched

it tightly. All three men listened to the beating of
distant hoofs.

"Split up!" Brom commanded. "He won't get away."

The three men spurred their horses in three different directions, through the Western Woods.

From the fourth direction came a deep rumble.

In a small house by the stable, little Tom Killian
heard the rumble, too. He was just finishing his sup-
per. Across the table, his father sat back contentedly
and began picking the food from between his teeth
with a knife.

As Tom's mother stood to clear plates, the table
began to shake. The glasses clinked together, the
dishes wobbled.

Tom hated thunder. He looked out the window
but saw no rain or lightning. Pushing himself back
from the table, he walked to the fireplace. From the
mantel, he took a tallow wick and lit it. Carrying it
close to him, he went into his bedroom. He sat on
the floor near his very favorite toy, a magic lantern.

With the tallow wick, he lit the inside wick of the
lantern. It burst into flame, casting bright light on
the glass outer sleeve, where the monsters were
painted. They glowed to life—cats screeching, dragons roaring, great slithery sea beasts. Tom turned the
lantern. The creatures danced across the walls of his
room, projected by the light.

"Rooooaaaaarr!" Tom growled. He felt much better.

In the kitchen, Beth Killian scolded her husband.
"Don't pick your teeth. You teach Thomas bad habits."

"I am a bad habit!" Mr. Killian pulled his wife
toward him playfully. "There's nothing for it."

"Oh, isn't there?"

As she leaned down to kiss her husband, she suddenly froze. The rumble had begun again, louder. The floor shook.

Killian put down his knife. His wife looked toward Tom's room.

With a sound like a gunshot, a kitchen window smacked open against the wall. A wind howled through the room, ferocious and loud. The entire house began to creak, as if a giant hand were shaking it.

Beth Killian's first thought was of Tom, how frightened he'd be. She dashed across the kitchen toward her son's room and swung open the door. But the boy was sitting on the floor, smiling, transfixed by the brightly colored monsters that danced across the walls.

Such a brave boy, she thought with relief.

Then, without warning, the animals stopped. Not the slightest movement, despite the violence of the wind. By rights, the lantern should have been whirling maniacally.

"Beth . . ." Mr. Killian called from the kitchen.

Mrs. Killian's smile vanished. Now the wind had ceased, with a silence abrupt and jarring.

For a moment all was still.

Slowly the creatures began to turn again as if by their own will, as if the laws of nature themselves had been turned inside out. They picked up speed until they dashed around the bedroom walls—wildly, frantically, in defiance of the utter stillness.

Mrs. Killian grabbed her son and ran toward the bedroom door. A blast of brightness made her stop short.

A blinding light exploded from the hearth, washing the room a harsh white. The flames twined and circled, transforming into shapes, until it seemed that a crowd of ghostly demon faces were dancing around in the fire. Mr. Killian backed away, staring.

CRRRRACK! A two-sided ax sliced through the front door.

Killian staggered backward. "Beth—run!" he cried out.

His wife disappeared into the bedroom. The door slammed shut.

Killian was alone. He turned toward the dark, hulking figure that barged through the shattered front door: a headless Hessian soldier, carrying an ax in each hand.

"Get out!" Killian shouted, but his words were feeble in the moaning wind.

The Horseman swung his ax.

Killian grabbed an iron skewer from the kitchen fireplace and held it out to block the blow.

At the impact, Killian fell back. But the Horseman swung again with the other ax.

Killian ducked. The blade sparked against the fireplace. It cracked a hearthstone in two.

As the Horseman recoiled, Killian's instincts took over. He thrust the skewer, full force. It pierced the Horseman's chest and emerged from his back.

Killian backed away in horror. The Horseman was still standing, still swinging. The flat of the ax caught Killian off guard. He jolted back against the wall, smacking his head.

With a mighty heave, the Horseman yanked the skewer out of his own body. He threw it to the floor and strode toward Killian.

Lifting the man by the hair, he drew back his ax and swung.

Dead.
He's dead.
The Headless Horseman came, and killed him.
Tom couldn't speak. He couldn't say the words he knew were true, but he had heard it all.

His mother was scared. She was kicking aside the bedroom rug, uncovering the little trapdoor, the one he was always afraid of. It led to the crawl space under the house where the mice and bugs lived.

But it would be all right now. Any place was better than the house.

She lifted him and lowered him into the space. He tried to stop sobbing but he couldn't.

"Hush, hush," Mother said. "Quiet as a mouse, now."

But what about Father? "Mother . . ."

"You must hide," she said.

He tucked himself in, but he was almost too big. Where would Mother fit? He jammed himself tightly into a corner, but Mother wasn't even coming down. She was still above, closing the door, not even trying.

She was all alone, with *him*.

Tom heard the bedroom door open. Through the cracks in the floorboards he saw a shadow of a man, holding something heavy in his hand.

"AAAAAGGGHHHHH!"

Mother.

Through the floorboards, he could see her fall to the floor. He could make out the patterns on her dress. And he could hear an object rolling dully across the room.

The object came to rest over a gap in the floor. Hair, soft and familiar, hung limply down from above.

Tom rolled up into a ball and closed his eyes as the ax began breaking through the floor above him.

11

AS BROM RODE OUT OF THE WOODS, HE SPOTTED THE horse immediately. It was unmistakably Daredevil, waiting by the house of the stableman, Killian. Brom's heart leaped. Kicking his own horse, he picked up speed.

Killian's front door swung open, sending a column of hearth light into the night. Through the door walked the Headless Horseman. Over his shoulder he carried a sack with three conspicuous bulges, two large, one small.

Brom shuddered. He was too late. The beast had struck and killed the whole family.

Now the Horseman was leaping onto Daredevil. He was heading back to his lair, his job finished—for now. But Brom knew that when the Hessian thirsted again, he'd return, and no one would be immune to his savagery, not even women and children.

Never again, Hessian. Not if Brom Van Brunt has any say in the matter.

Brom took his own horse's reins in his mouth. He raised his rifle and aimed.

Direct hit. His bullet ripped through the Horseman, knocking him to the ground. The black horse took off at a gallop.

Brom sped toward the house. He pulled up on the reins, stopping just short of the body, which lay chest-down in tatters, smoldering. The monster hadn't been as invincible as everyone thought, or perhaps not as smart.

At any rate, he hadn't counted on the likes of me. With a triumphant grin, Brom dismounted and walked toward his kill.

Then the body twitched, slowly rising to its feet.

Brom stopped. Dropping to one knee, he fumbled for his rifle and powder horn. The Hessian was alive. This was impossible. The shot had blasted him open. No man could have survived that.

Unsheathing his sword, the Horseman approached. Brom could see the gunshot wound, the shredded flesh and exposed viscera.

No man indeed. He is no man.

"Yeeeeeaaaagh!" Brom bellowed, pointing his rifle at the advancing figure.

But the Hessian was swift. He swung his sword in a tight arc toward Brom's head.

CLANK.

Brom fended off the blow with his rifle, but the Horseman charged relentlessly.

CLANK. CLANK. CLANK.

All Brom could do was block—and pray.

As Ichabod emerged from the wood, he heard the clashing metal. He saw the bloodied, bullet-torn Horseman swing an ax upward, connecting with Brom's rifle, sending it skyward. He saw Brom fall to the ground, defenseless. Even at this distance, Brom's face projected the fear of death.

Sleepy Hollow

The village was a quiet, unremarkable place. *A bit too quiet,* Ichabod thought.

At the Van Tassels' party the blindfolded young woman embraced Ichabod. "Have a kiss on account," she said mischievously.

Then Ichabod turned to meet his hosts, Baltus Van Tassel and his wife.

Ichabod began his investigation by putting on a pair of glasses fitted with magnifying lenses.

Masbath's son stood near the grave marker, his shoulders sunken with a sadness greater than his youth deserved.

The body of the Widow Winship was laid out in
Dr. Lancaster's medical room. "I shall need to operate,"
Ichabod told the doctor.

Katrina was reading a slim, well-worn book. "Take
this," she told Ichabod. "It is my gift to you."

Baltus Van Tassel summoned Reverend Steenwyck, Notary Hardenbrook, and Dr. Lancaster. "This time I'll go to New York myself," Baltus declared, "and I won't be fobbed off with an amateur deductor."

Ichabod circled the Tree of the Dead until he found the Horseman's sword. It was his grave marker, rusted and entangled with twenty years' growth of roots.

*N*ever *again,*
Hessian, Brom
vowed as he
walked toward
the fallen body of
the Horseman.

*I*chabod struggled through the panicked crowd in the church. "Stop this!" he cried. "The Horseman cannot enter the church!"

The Horseman was thundering up the hill. He would be upon the windmill in seconds.

As the Horseman hacked at the windmill's trapdoor, Ichabod formed a plan of escape for Katrina and Young Masbath.

The Tree of the Dead

But the Horseman did not advance. Instead, he turned and walked away.

Just as he had veered away from the three of us in the woods. He didn't want us. He doesn't want Brom. He picks his victims.

The Horseman did not kill indiscriminately. He had a motive. Find it, and Ichabod might be able to determine the next victim. With that information, hope was possible. Perhaps a plan for capture could be made.

Now Brom was pulling a dagger from his belt and rising to his feet.

The fool. Ichabod spurred Gunpowder toward him, but Brom took no notice. He heaved the dagger, and with a sickening thud it lodged in the Hessian's back.

The Horseman turned, the tip of the weapon jutting from his chest. He grabbed the blade and ripped the dagger out from the front.

His face taut with fear, Brom leaped to his feet and ran.

The Horseman threw. The knife whipped through the air and lodged in Brom's thigh. With a scream, Brom fell. The Horseman strode toward him, lifting his sword.

Ichabod dug his feet into Gunpowder's side. *Go—GO, you nag!*

The Hessian's foot was on Brom's back, holding him to the ground. Ichabod reached for his lantern, swung it around . . . *only a few more yards . . .*

Gripping the sword with both hands, blade down, the Hessian lifted it high above Brom.

Now.

Ichabod swung the lantern. He caught the Horseman broadside, knocking him to the ground.

Brom staggered to his feet. Limping badly, he dragged himself into Killian's barn. Ichabod jumped off Gunpowder and ran after him.

As the Horseman rose, Brom emerged from the barn door, brandishing two long, sharp scythes. But the Horseman was turning, walking away again, toward Daredevil.

Brom suddenly dropped a scythe and snatched Ichabod's pistol.

"Wait! Don't you see?" Ichabod said, grabbing Brom's arm. "He's not after us!"

Brom wasn't listening. He shook loose, aimed, and fired. The bullet smacked into the Horseman's back. His flesh exploded, spitting outward along with shreds of his uniform. He lurched forward a bit, then slowly turned.

"He is now," Ichabod murmured.

Brom flung the pistol aside. Stooping down, he grabbed the scythes.

Out of the corner of his eye, Ichabod spotted movement. Two figures on horseback emerged from the woods—Theodore and Glen, Brom's friends. For a moment he hoped they'd join the fight; perhaps with their help, the beast could be subdued. But the two men instantly fled.

Now the Hessian was attacking with ax and sword. Brom deflected each blow with a scythe.

Ichabod ducked into the barn and fetched a sharp sickle. Raising it high, he ran full-tilt toward the Horseman, who now advanced steadily on Brom, slashing with both arms.

The Horseman spun around, catching Ichabod's blow with his ax.

Ichabod reared back and charged again. Brom attacked from the other side, but the Hessian held his ground, his arms moving with swift assurance, parrying, deflecting, attacking.

Ichabod's sickle flew out of his hand, thrown by a sudden thrust of the Horseman's ax. The Hessian then turned fully on Brom, sword and ax slashing with vicious accuracy. With equal skill, Brom caught both weapons in his scythes.

The Horseman was immobilized. He and Brom stood locked, an arm's length from each other. For a long, excruciating moment, nothing happened.

Then the Hessian kicked.

Brom went flying. He landed and rolled, grabbing Ichabod's sickle. Springing to his feet, he leaped toward the Horseman and swung.

Thud.

The sickle sank into the Horseman's torso.

"Now you've annoyed him," Ichabod said.

The monster struggled with the embedded blade, lurching right and left. The handle slammed Ichabod in the jaw and he shot backward, hitting the ground with a jolt. Brom pulled him to his feet.

"We cannot win this!" Ichabod pleaded.

Even Brom knew this now. Running was the only option, but not without protection. Brom grabbed the scythes, Ichabod pulled a wood-splitting ax from a tree stump, and both men sped toward the covered bridge on foot.

A plan, Ichabod thought. *We must have a plan.* But he couldn't think straight. He could only feel. And what he felt was utter panic.

Just before the bridge, Brom's leg buckled. His wound was trailing blood. Ichabod offered his arm.

Brom held onto him for support as they entered the bridge shed.

Behind them the Horseman's footsteps approached, loud and heavy. He had shaken off the sickle somehow. Ichabod tried to pull Brom faster, but Brom was grimacing with pain, his limp growing worse by the moment.

We'll never make it.

The footsteps were right behind them, and then they changed. They were hollower, odd sounding.

Ichabod looked up. The Horseman was *above* them, his boots thudding along the roof of the covered bridge.

At the other end, the Horseman leaped down. He spun in midair and landed in a crouch to face them.

Ichabod stopped short. The Hessian's hulking form filled the exit. Slowly, he stepped into the bridge shed.

Ichabod let go of Brom. Taking his ax in both hands, he lunged forward and struck. With a quick upward stroke of his battle-ax, the Horseman split Ichabod's ax handle in two. He headed for Brom now, bringing his sword down hard.

Ichabod's instincts took over. He pulled Brom out of the blade's path, but he felt the sword enter his shoulder and slice through to his back.

"AAAAAAGGHHH!"

The Horseman yanked the sword upward. Ichabod left the ground, still at the end of the blade. As he fell to the wooden floor, the sword slid out.

Ichabod clutched his shoulder, writhing in agony. His field of vision was spotted with red. He struggled to focus through the pain. Brom was upright on shaky legs, clutching both scythes.

The Horseman walked steadily forward. His arms moved with speed and precision, striking, chopping, thrusting.

Brom backpedaled, blocking the barrage, his face distorted with terror.

All Ichabod could see now was the Horseman's back. All he could hear was the steady clank—clank—clank of metal upon metal as Brom defended himself.

Ichabod struggled to stand, to move forward, to distract the Horseman. But his legs gave way, and as he thumped to the floor, the steady clanking gave way to a different sound: a sickening thud, followed by another and another.

The Horseman was standing over Brom now, hacking away like a woodsman. When he was finished, he turned toward Ichabod.

Ichabod's eyes blurred. He never expected death to arrive like this.

But the Horseman walked steadily past him, back toward his horse. He left the remains of Brom Van Brunt in a grisly heap on the wooden floor.

It was the last image Ichabod saw before he passed out.

12

"REMARKABLE. A WOUND LIKE THIS SHOULD HAVE killed him. But it needs no stitch, and there's hardly any loss of blood."

Ichabod recognized the voice of Dr. Lancaster

through a haze of half-consciousness. Struggling to open his eyes, he felt weak, cold, clammy with sweat. Pain coursed through his body, radiating from his shoulder down.

Lancaster slowly came into focus. So did Baltus Van Tassel.

Ichabod was in his own bedroom at the Van Tassel manor. Night had fallen; the room was lit by candle-light.

"He stirs," Baltus said.

I live. Brom is dead. The Horseman escaped. Where is Katrina? Is she safe?

Ichabod tried to sit up but collapsed backward.

"You must be still," Dr. Lancaster warned. "The fever is on you."

The fever didn't matter. His life didn't matter. Only one thing did.

"Katrina . . ." he mumbled.

In the Van Tassel kitchen, Katrina bent over the giant hearth. On the brick floor was a knife and a dead crow, its foot cut off. A beaker was suspended over the flame, and it began to bubble, green leaves roiling vigorously in a milky white substance.

"*Nostradamus mediamus, milk of mercy in media nos laudamus,*" she chanted. "*Nostradamus mediamus, milk of mercy in media nos laudamus . . .*"

She repeated the chant exactly the required number of times. That was crucial. Then she deftly removed the beaker from the fire and placed it on a plate to cool. When the potion reached the right temperature, she walked it up to Ichabod's room.

Her father and Dr. Lancaster were in there, leaning over Ichabod, trying to force-feed him a vile-looking green medicine.

"It will restore you," Dr. Lancaster pleaded.

Ichabod's mouth was sealed tightly—and rightly so, Katrina thought. The doctor's remedies were useless.

Katrina sat by the side of Ichabod's bed. He glanced at her through watery, fear-stricken eyes. His skin was wan, his hair matted. When he spoke, his voice was thin and parched. "I—I tried to stop Brom, but—"

"Sssssh," Katrina said. "No one could have done more. Drink this down. It will make you sleep."

"The Horseman was not set to kill Brom—or me. . . . If Brom had not attacked him—"

"Later," Baltus said. "Rest now."

But Ichabod pressed on. "I have discovered something—"

"These are ravings," Baltus murmured to Dr. Lancaster.

"The Horseman does not kill for the sake of killing," Ichabod insisted. "He chooses his victims!"

"Drink," Katrina said.

She held the beaker to Ichabod's lips. He drank the potion down in one gulp, then fell to the pillow, unconscious.

Katrina sat back. Her father leaned forward, his face lined with concern and trepidation.

Behind her the door opened, and Lady Van Tassel walked into the room. "What is it, Baltus?" she asked, reaching down for her husband's hand.

"Nothing, nothing," he replied. "Don't be troubled, my dear."

Ichabod's eyes were flickering under the lids now.

Good, Katrina thought. Ichabod was dreaming. Perhaps, for a while, he would no longer ache.

He is in a place of God, a church, but he feels no comfort, just terror.

It is nighttime. In the light of his lantern, the statues cast deep shadows that seem to follow him.

He is looking for something . . . someone . . .

He hears a sound behind him.

He drops between pews. Douses his lantern. He must not be seen.

Across the church, a red door swings open. It is Father. He's with another man, the ugly one who took Mother away. They are talking softly, and he can't hear the words. The man is holding a piece of parchment. They head into the church.

Ichabod crouches low. He can smell the mud on the man's boots as they pass and the faint aroma of incense on Father's clothes. Then they are gone through the front door.

Ichabod is alone . . . maybe.

He stands and walks to the red door. The entrance to the secret room. A voice is telling him no, but he will not listen because he has to see.

He opens the door. A shaft of early-morning light breaks through a stained-glass window, faintly lighting the objects within.

He has always imagined what might be in the room—robes and incense burners, candles and statues, icons.

But his image is wrong. None of those things are here. Instead of paintings, iron cuffs hang from the wall. Long knifes lie on a table and sharp needles and an enormous corkscrew. Against the wall is a spiked chair.

"For every crime there must be a punishment"— Father's words. But these? Here?

He feels weak. He stumbles back a step.

Then he sees the coffin.

Only it's not a coffin, more like a sarcophagus, standing upright, shut with a padlock. It's made of solid metal except for a slit at face level.

And through that slit, illuminated by the column of light, are two eyes, eyes he knows well, eyes that have always looked upon him with kindness and happiness and love. Now they stare straight ahead, blank and lifeless.

He has found Mother.

A scream rings out. He's aware of it, but he doesn't know it's coming from his own throat, and he's banging, banging, clawing at the lock, trying to pry it open, to reverse what has happened (*my fault, it's my fault, she reached for me but I let her go*), and the eyes stare back uncomprehending and flat, and he finally has to turn away, falling to the floor in a pool of his own tears, knowing that the pain is too much, *too much;* he'll surely explode.

The chair is in front of him, the spikes glinting in the dusty sunlight.

He reaches up. He places his palms on the thick clusters of spikes. Where his skin touches, blood begins to spill.

He presses down, hard. The spikes open deep, long gashes in his skin.

And he no longer feels the pain.

13

"AHHHHH!"

Ichabod jolted upward. Two arms caught him and held him—Katrina's.

"Hush, hush," she whispered. "You were dreaming."

She was taking out a handkerchief now and dabbing it on his palms. Tiny rivulets of blood flowed from his scars, the scars he had never quite understood, until . . .

"Yes," Ichabod said, "things I had forgotten and would not like to remember."

"Perhaps the remembering is the hard road to peace of mind," Katrina replied. "What ails you, Ichabod?"

"I was well—it was the world that was ill. But since I came here—"

"You were not a happy man when you came. I think your wound was deeper than the wound you received from the Horseman." Katrina touched the back of her palm to Ichabod's forehead. "But your fever is broken, and though I cannot cure the world, I would make you live happy in it. Tell me what you dreamed."

"How I found my mother dead. How good and evil sometimes wear each other's clothes. She was an innocent, a child of nature, condemned—*murdered* by my father."

"Murdered by—"

"Yes. Murdered to save her soul—by a Bible-black tyrant behind a mask of righteousness. I was seven when I lost my faith."

"What *do* you believe in, Ichabod?"

"Sense and reason, cause and consequence, an ordered universe. Oh, lord, I should not have come to this place where my rational mind has been so controverted by the spirit world."

Katrina nodded sadly. "Is there nothing you will take from Sleepy Hollow that was worth the coming here?"

"No, nothing." Ichabod looked her in the eye. "A kiss—and how rare a thing—a kiss from a lovely woman before she saw my face or knew my name."

"Yes. Without sense or reason." Katrina leaned closer. "It was a kiss on account."

On account. And now, perhaps, the chance to fulfill the debt . . .

Ichabod suddenly pulled away. "Oh—God forgive me—I talk of kisses, and you have lost your brave man, Brom!"

"I have shed my tears for Brom," Katrina replied. "And yet my heart is not broken. Do you think me wicked?"

"No. But perhaps there is a little bit of a witch in you, Katrina."

"Why do you say that?"

Her eyes were pleading. Probing to find the place where rationality ended and emotion began.

Say it, Crane. Tell her.

"Because," he said, "you have bewitched me."

As they embraced, the dark dream faded, and Ichabod no longer noticed the blood on his hands.

Downstairs, in a small servant's room, Young Masbath sat up in bed.

Since his father's death, he hadn't slept soundly. The world, to him, no longer promised safety or sense. Even the smallest noises roused him. Tonight it was the footsteps outside the house.

He peered out his window. The soft light of a lantern swung in an arc on the lawn. It was carried by a cloaked figure walking quietly toward town.

Quickly Young Masbath dressed, left the house, and followed.

The morning, like all others in this godforsaken place, was gray and gloomy. Ichabod awakened at the sound of his bedroom door opening.

Katrina.

He sat up expectantly, but the visitor was Lady Van Tassel, carrying a tray of food and drink.

"You slept like the dead," she remarked.

Ichabod modestly pulled up his covers. "You are too kind to me. I do not look to be served by the lady of the house."

"Nor would you, but that the servant girl has vanished."

"Sarah?"

"Run away, like many more. People are leaving in fear, without ceremony."

"Where is—"

He stopped himself from saying Katrina's name, cautious about betraying his feelings.

"She watched over you till dawn," Lady Van Tassel

said, turning toward the door. "Now it is her turn to sleep."

She knew; she seemed to see everything. As she left, Ichabod felt himself blush.

Young Masbath bustled into the room and began preparing Ichabod's clothes and washing basin.

"Help me," Ichabod said. "I am fit for another day, I think."

"Where are we going?" Young Masbath asked softly.

"To the notary's office."

"Why?"

"Because that is where I expect to find deposited the last will and testament of the elder Van Garrett."

"You have thought of something!" Young Masbath said.

"Of something *you* said, Young Masbath: 'The Widow Winship came many a day with a basket of eggs to Van Garrett.' "

The statement had struck Ichabod as incongruous, for a reason he could not fathom—until he remembered words Katrina had told him: "When my father brought us to Sleepy Hollow, Van Garrett set him up with an acre and a broken-down cottage, a dozen of Van Garrett hens."

"Van Garrett, I understand, had hens to spare," Ichabod went on.

The boy's face clouded. Ichabod could see he had caught on—the eggs had been a pretext. The widow had another reason for visiting. She and Van Garrett were in love.

"I begin to see . . ." Ichabod went on. "It was Van Garrett's child that the widow was carrying! And what news have you?"

Young Masbath gestured grimly out the window. "I heard someone leaving last night. Looked like they headed to town, but I lost them in the woods."

A suspect. But to what crime? How did this connect to the Horseman? "You didn't see who?"

"All I saw was the lantern," Young Masbath replied as he fetched a clean shirt for Ichabod.

Into the woods. Into the lair of the Horseman at dark, where no one in his right mind would dare to go. Unless . . .

Unless the person had no reason to fear.

Yes. The pieces were beginning to fall together. "The Horseman does the killing," Ichabod mused aloud as he quickly dressed for the day's work, "but, I believe, at the bidding of a mortal, someone of flesh and blood."

"What makes you say that?" Young Masbath asked.

"The witch—the crone—when I happened upon her corpse, she lay in a pool of blood. Blood poured hard from her neck. *The wound was not cauterized!*"

"Then . . . she was not killed by the Hessian. Someone only tried to make it *seem* so."

Ichabod nodded. "It was the settling of a private score. But the Horseman cuts heads to a different drum. The crone pointed us to what drives the Hessian—his skull has been stolen from his grave. The person who stole it has power over him. Here is why the Headless One has returned through the fate of the Tree of the Dead—*he chops heads until his own is restored to him!*"

"But what person—"

"A person who stands to gain by these murders."

* * *

The banging of hammers and the smell of sawdust greeted Ichabod and Young Masbath as they rode into town. In house after house, men boarded up windows. Occasionally, upon seeing Ichabod, they spoke in hushed tones and glowered angrily.

A crowd stood in front of the general store. Inside, people handed them provisions to be conveyed hand over hand to nearby wheelbarrows, which others then pushed toward the church.

Not far from there stood Notary Hardenbrook's office. Ichabod and Young Masbath dismounted and tied their horses to the post. They watched the stream of townspeople heading toward the old church, jamming the gate of the wrought-iron fence that surrounded it. On the grounds, a group worked to erect large wooden crosses.

"Sanctuary," Ichabod remarked. "Or so they hope."

Reverend Steenwyck's strident voice cut through the bustle. He stood on a crate in front of the church, pointing to Ichabod. "There he is! There! The desecrator of Christian burial! Twice he met the Horseman and kept his head! How is it so? *The devil protects his own!*"

A thick clot of dirt smacked against Ichabod's shoulder. He grabbed Young Masbath and rushed into Hardenbrook's office.

The old man barely looked up as they entered. Every inch of the room was crammed with papers, as if not one sheet had ever been moved since the day he opened business. The place smelled of ink, mildew, and neglect.

"I take it, Mr. Hardenbrook," Ichabod said,

preparing for a fight, "that wills and testaments are
held here on public record?"

Hardenbrook sullenly handed him a legal docu-
ment. "I believe this is what you wish to see. Take it
and go!"

Ichabod was stunned. Hardenbrook had given up
easily. Why? As he carefully perused the yellowed
sheet, Ichabod could not stop his fingers from trembling. The heading was set in clear, plain type:

LAST WILL AND TESTAMENT

PETER VAN GARRETT

"Van Garrett Senior left his estate to his next of
kin," Hardenbrook explained, "that is to say, to his
only son. However, the son being murdered in the
same instant—"

"The next of kin after the son would be the eldest
of the line from Van Garrett's father's sister," Ichabod
deduced, the line of succession instantly becoming
clear. "None other than Baltus Van Tassel, something
no one else thought to mention!"

Baltus. It didn't seem possible.

"Well, you have found your way to it," Hardenbrook snapped, "and I hope you will leave now, before my windows are broken."

"I am not ready to leave," Ichabod declared.

Hardenbrook let out a moan.

"A brick through your window is not what puts
you in terror, Hardenbrook. There is something else.
I saw your fear—and Steenwyck's and the doctor's—
when you met at Philipse's house. Philipse paid with
his head, and you fear for your own."

"Yes, it's true!" Hardenbrook shouted. "But we did

not know it was a murdering plot when we were drawn in!"

"Drawn in by whom?" Ichabod pressed.

Hardenbrook sagged in his seat, wringing his hands. "Mercy upon me . . . we meant no harm to come to her . . ."

"No harm to come to whom?"

"But the marriage made her next of kin . . ."

"Made *who* next of kin to *whom?* I'm confused."

"He means," Young Masbath spoke up, "that old Van Garrett secretly married the Widow Winship."

It all made sense now. The widow was Van Garrett's wife. She would inherit the estate.

"Of course!" Ichabod said. "And Van Garrett must have made a new will, leaving everything to her—so she stood between Baltus and the legacy! Where is the new will?"

"I cannot be seen to help you," Hardenbrook pleaded. "The Horseman will come for me!"

"I will not leave without the very last will and testament of—"

Hardenbrook abruptly tore into a pile of papers, tossing the top sheets into the air. Papers flew at Ichabod's feet as the old man dug deeper and deeper until finally he flung another will at Ichabod. "Go, then! I am a dead man!"

Hardenbrook's features seemed to sink inward. He buried his face, sobbing uncontrollably.

"Sir?" Young Masbath said.

Ichabod scanned the paper quickly. An unexpected signature at the bottom made his heart drop: Jonathan Masbath.

"Young Masbath . . ." Ichabod said slowly, a new and painful detail revealing itself. "I know why your father died. That night when Van Garrett quarreled with his son, Jonathan Masbath was summoned upstairs to witness the new will. Here is your father's signature. It was his death warrant."

Young Masbath took the sheet. His eyes welled up as he looked at the familiar script.

Looking down, Ichabod spotted another set of names, on a sheet near his left shoe. He stooped to pick it up and scanned the text. "The marriage certificate! Parson Steenwyck married Van Garrett and Widow Winship."

It was all falling into place now. A little logic revealed how the other men fit in.

"Dr. Lancaster confirmed the widow was pregnant," Ichabod said. "She told the secret to Magistrate Philipse. Notary Hardenbrook concealed the documents—and you all kept silence! Why? For some nameless dread of the man who stood to gain by it—Baltus Van Tassel!"

The ride home was swift. As Ichabod and Young Masbath started up the stairs to Ichabod's room, they spotted a light through a crack in the parlor door. Inside, Baltus sat hunched over a table, sipping from a half-empty liquor glass and intent on a large, open chest before him. He was oblivious to the two sets of watching eyes as he reached into the chest for a fistful of silver coins. Carefully he let them flow, one by one, into a pile on the table.

So close-lipped. So smooth.

Of all the characters Ichabod had met, Baltus was the last he would have suspected—despite his years of experience as New York City constable, which had taught him to trust no one. Perhaps he had simply not wanted to suspect. Baltus had been good to him.

"I think," Young Masbath whispered, climbing up behind Ichabod, "that there is some error in your reasoning."

"Really?" Ichabod replied. "Do give me the benefit of your—"

"All these murders, just so that Baltus Van Tassel should inherit yet more land and property?"

"Precisely. Men murder for profit. Possibly you don't know New York?"

At the top of the stairs Ichabod turned toward his bedroom. The door was ajar. Quietly he walked to it and peered in. Katrina was sitting at his desk, reading his ledger.

"Katrina," Ichabod said. "What are you doing in my room?"

Katrina turned with a start. "Because," she said, catching her breath, "it is *yours*. Is it wicked of me?"

"No . . ." Ichabod replied tentatively. Wicked, no. Odd, yes.

"I missed you. Where did you go?"

"To the notary. I had questions to ask Hardenbrook."

"And did you learn anything of interest?"

"Well . . . perhaps."

He gave Young Masbath a wary glance. Of course, they could not tell her. She must not find out until they knew more.

Katrina's expression grew grim. "My father thinks you should return to New York."

Naturally. He suspects we're onto him. "Really?" Ichabod said. "Why is that?"

"I don't know." Katrina smiled ruefully. "Perhaps

he looked in your ledger and did not like what he saw."

Ichabod stepped over to see the open book. He remembered the page. On it was a sketch he'd drawn of Katrina. It was surrounded by her name, written over and over in rococo variations. His face reddening, he quickly shut the ledger.

"He believes townsfolk and country do not mix," Katrina explained.

Opening the desk drawer, Ichabod slipped in the Van Garrett will and marriage certificate.

"What have you there?" Katrina asked.

"Evidence," Ichabod replied. "I'm sorry, I must ask for privacy."

Katrina retreated to the door. "Then I will leave you to your thoughts. Sleep well."

As she left, Ichabod's eye caught a sudden movement. A shadow skittered across the floor, spindly and silent. A rat this size would not have fazed Ichabod. But this was something far more fearsome—a spider. He screamed, leaping away, as it skittered under his bed.

Young Masbath gave him a curious glance. "It's only a spider."

"Where's it gone? Where's it gone? Can you see it?"

Young Masbath crouched and looked under the bed. His brow creased. "There's something under here."

"Kill it! Kill It!" *Get a hold of yourself, Crane!* "No. No. Er, *stun* it."

Young Masbath grabbed one end of the bed. "Help me move the bed."

Ichabod pulled the other end, and the bed slid away from the wall. On the floor, drawn in chalk, was a strange figure, a five-sided star inside a circle: a pentagram.

The spider sat in the center of it.

"Look!" Young Masbath cried out. "The Evil Eye! It is someone casting spells against you!"

The eerie shape merged in Ichabod's vision with the loathsome black creature. "The Evil Eye . . ." he murmured.

Sleeping that night was out of the question.

Ichabod's mind reeled. He had erased the drawing under the bed as well as he could. He had told himself it was only a silly magic symbol—but still, it bothered him.

He heard the parlor clock strike twelve times. Midnight. The same time at which Young Masbath had seen the mysterious person escape into the woods the night before.

His heart skipped when he heard a floorboard creak downstairs. He kicked Young Masbath, who had fallen asleep on his floor. The boy bolted upright. At the sound of the next creak, he reached for a lantern.

Together they sneaked downstairs as somewhere in the house a door opened and closed. Someone was leaving.

They followed the sound outside. Far ahead of them, holding a lantern, a hooded figure walked toward the woods across the covered bridge.

Keeping the lantern in sight, Ichabod and Young Masbath stayed safely behind. As they entered the Western Woods, the tree cover blocked all light.

They had to feel before them with their arms, watching for the amber glow.

Soon the lantern disappeared over a small ridge, and they heard voices.

"Wait here," Ichabod whispered. He climbed the ridge alone and carefully peeked over the top.

The lantern was on a granite rock. It cast a circle of light over two people. One was a man. The other was the person Ichabod and Young Masbath had been following. He could see now that it was a woman.

As the couple kissed passionately in the light, Ichabod moved forward.

The woman's hood fell back, and as she looked up, smiling, Ichabod caught a clear glimpse of Lady Van Tassel's face.

With her was the last man Ichabod would have expected: Reverend Steenwyck.

As Steenwyck kissed her, frantically, feverishly, Lady Van Tassel raised a knife behind his back.

Ichabod tensed, ready to rush forward, but he stopped himself. Lady Van Tassel was cutting her own hand, drawing the knife across her palm.

She lifted Reverend Steenwyck's shirt, smearing the blood over his back. Ichabod felt ill. He backed quickly down the ridge.

"What was there?" Young Masbath asked.

"Something I wish I had not seen," Ichabod replied, heading back.

Young Masbath was curious but soon stopped asking questions. The walk back was blundering and slow, and it took all their attention.

Ichabod was exhausted by the time they reached the house. His legs hurt as he walked inside and trudged up the stairs. But he snapped to attention the moment they walked into the bedroom.

His desk drawer was open. The Van Garrett papers were gone.

14

"SHE WILL NOT SEE YOU," LADY VAN TASSEL SAID with a sympathetic shrug.

Ichabod had waited up all night. He had heard Lady Van Tassel sneaking in before dawn. With a straight face, he had come down to the kitchen and waited until Lady Van Tassel emerged for breakfast preparations. Then he had politely asked for an audience with Katrina.

Ichabod paced the kitchen floor, straining not to stare at Lady Van Tassel's bandaged hand. Nothing made sense, especially what he'd seen in the woods. Lady Van Tassel and Reverend Steenwyck? Why?

Ichabod shook off the thought. He had to speak with Katrina. The important thing was getting his papers back. "Did she say anything?"

"Only that she will not come down."

"I see. Thank you." Exasperated, Ichabod turned to leave.

"Constable," Lady Van Tassel called out, "you have not asked me how I hurt my hand since yesterday, which would have been polite. In fact, you have been as careful not to look at it as not to mention it."

She unwrapped the bandage, revealing a long cut on her palm, stitched roughly together.

"Yes, I'm sorry," Ichabod said. "How did you—"

Lady Van Tassel grabbed him by the wrist and pulled him close. "I know you saw me," she whispered.

"What?"

"I know you followed me last night. You must promise not to tell my husband what you saw. Promise me!"

Ichabod tried to pull loose, but her grip was firm. He heard the front door slam. Footsteps approached.

"Reverend Steenwyck has power over me," Lady Van Tassel said.

"P-p-power?" Ichabod stammered.

"He knows something terrible against my dear husband. What you witnessed was the price of Steenwyck's silence."

"What does Steenwyck know?"

Just then the door handle turned. "Later," Lady Van Tassel whispered, releasing Ichabod. "Later."

Baltus barged into the room, heading straight for the liquor. "The town is in a ferment. Horror piled on tragedy. Hardenbrook is dead—strangled!"

Lady Van Tassel gasped. "That harmless old man?"

Hardenbrook, the man who knew. The man whose records betrayed Baltus.

As Baltus poured himself a drink, Ichabod couldn't help watching his hands close around the neck of the bottle—strong, thick, farmer's hands. They were hands that could easily choke a man to death.

"Hanged himself in the night!" Baltus said. "Reverend Steenwyck has called a meeting at the church, tonight. Every man, woman, and child." He turned to Ichabod. "He will speak against you. If you are wise, you will be gone from here. Steenwyck's congregation is already halfway to being a mob."

"I will go when I have done what I came to do," Ichabod said.

Baltus's face darkened. Quickly Lady Van Tassel placed a comforting arm on her husband's shoulder.

He glanced at her bandage. "What is this?"

"I was careless with the kitchen knife," Lady Van Tassel replied.

"The wound looks angry."

"I'll bind it later with wild arrowroot flowers. I know where I'll find some. Will you ride with me?"

Ichabod slipped out, leaving the two alone. He ran straight upstairs to Katrina's room.

If she won't come to me, I'll go to her.

He rapped on the door, but there was no answer. Quietly, he pushed his way in. The opening door made the fireplace ashes swirl. They were black: wispy-thin ashes of paper, not wood.

Ichabod groaned. His case was vanishing; he could never recover those documents now. And Katrina was gone.

Young Masbath darted into the room, breathless. "I saw her riding away," he said, "toward the old pasture."

Ichabod took the stairs two at a time.

Inside the old windmill, on a hill at the edge of the Van Tassel field, a cloaked figure crouched by a burning pile of straw.

With gloved hands, the figure unfolded a sheet of

paper, then lifted it high over the flames. Out spilled strands of hair, which shriveled into dust as they fell into the fire.

Reaching into a cloth bag, the figure pulled out a large human skull, then carefully placed it in the center of the flame.

In the dancing blaze, it seemed to grin. Its teeth were oddly sharp. They had been honed to points.

Ichabod ran through the Western Woods. His sense of direction had become quite keen, and soon he reached the spot where he'd hoped to find Katrina.

She was exactly where he thought she'd be, at the abandoned cottage, the place where he'd seen her first conjuring magic. She was crouched over the ruins of the hearth, chanting over a small fire, mumbling magic spells. Her horse grazed peacefully nearby.

"Katrina," Ichabod called out.

She turned and stood. Her face was red, her eyes angry, and her cheeks streaked with tears.

"You took the papers and burned them?" Ichabod asked.

"So that you would not have them to accuse my father," Katrina replied.

"I—I accuse no one. But if there is guilt, I cannot alter it, no matter how much it grieves me. And no spells of yours can alter it either."

"If you knew my father, you would not have such harsh thoughts about him—no, nor if you felt anything for me!"

The words hurt. Ichabod wanted to comfort her, but what could he possibly say? How could he ease the pain of knowledge of a father corrupted by greed? "I am pinioned by a chain of reasoning! Why else did his four friends conspire to conceal?"

"You are the constable, not I. So find another chain of reasoning and let me be!"

"I cannot—not one or the other. I am heartsick with it."

"I think you have no heart—and I had a mind once to give you mine!"

She whirled toward her horse. As she mounted, it reared up, its front legs pawing the air over Ichabod's head.

"Yes, I think you loved me that day when you followed me into the Western Woods," Ichabod cried out. "To have braved such peril!"

"What peril was there for me, if it was my own father who controlled the Headless Horseman?" Katrina retorted. "Good-bye, Ichabod Crane! I curse the day you came to Sleepy Hollow!"

She rode away before he could answer.

At dusk the deep, steady sound of church bells reached the edge of the field, where Baltus waited on his horse impatiently. He could see his wife through a copse, searching through the underbrush.

At least she was in sight. He'd lost her for a while. She was taking an awfully long time. "Come!" he called out. "Hurry up! The meeting bell has started tolling!"

What on earth was she doing, picking the arrowroot petals one by one? He glanced impatiently toward the town, gauging how long it would take to return.

Looking back toward his wife, he went pale.

Out of the woods rode the Horseman on a steady path to Lady Van Tassel—the headless after the heedless. The Horseman was unsheathing his sword.

Ichabod lurked in the shadowed crannies of the town square, wearing a dark cloak and a wide-brimmed hat, to avoid the panicked throng. Having been brainwashed by Steenwyck, they all blamed him now. If one of them discovered his identity, they'd surely tar and feather him in public, if not worse.

When he spotted Katrina walking toward the church along with everyone else, he followed close behind.

The thundering of hooves made him turn toward the field.

Baltus was riding in—red-faced, frightened, nearly falling off his horse. "The Horseman! Save me!"

"Father?" Katrina called out.

Baltus leaped to the ground and clutched his daughter. "He killed her! The Horseman has killed your stepmother!"

He was frantic, panicked.

This is not the demeanor of a man who consorts with ghosts.

A horse's angry screech trumpeted from within the woods, accompanied by the pounding of hoofbeats. All motion stopped, all eyes turned toward the sound.

As the Headless Horseman and his steed burst from the trees, pandemonium erupted. Those who were still in the streets sprinted toward the church, scrambling over one another to get through the gate.

The churchyard itself emptied as men abandoned the crosses they were building and ran inside.

Baltus was running, too, followed by his daughter—to the church, to sanctuary. It was ludicrous, Ichabod thought, to believe that the building would protect them. But there was possible safety in numbers—and now that Ichabod's entire case had just fallen apart, safety was all he could hope for.

He ran after them, followed by Young Masbath.

"I know what you are thinking," Ichabod said over his shoulder.

"It seems Baltus Van Tassel is not the one who controls the Headless Horseman," Young Masbath replied.

They were the last through the church door. It slammed shut on a scene of utter panic.

Women rushed children ahead of them into the church basement. Men grabbed rifles from stockpiles and stood on pews to look through holes in the boarded-up windows.

Ichabod rushed to a window and peered between the wooden planks. Outside, Daredevil screamed. He reared up on hind legs before the church gate, refusing to enter.

The Horseman yanked hard on the reins, trying to spur the horse through, but Daredevil held fast. Then, with a gesture so uncharacteristically gentle that it startled Ichabod, the Horseman tossed his ax underhanded into the churchyard, over the fence.

It disintegrated in the air, falling to the ground like dust.

Sanctuary.

It had worked. Ichabod was astonished.

Now he saw Katrina, storming across the church

amid the chaos. She glowered briefly at him, her face full of accusation. Then she flung herself on the altar, all her fear and despair bursting forth in a torrent of tears.

Ichabod stepped forward but flinched at the sound of musket shot.

The men were firing now, their weapons following the Headless Horseman as he circled outside the gate. Young Masbath grabbed a gun and joined them.

Through the window, Ichabod saw bullets tearing into the flesh of the Hessian and his horse. Calmly, unfazed, the pair turned and headed into the town square.

When Ichabod looked back, Katrina was gone, lost in the crush of people. He looked around frantically and caught sight of Reverend Steenwyck, racing toward the cellar door. There, Baltus Van Tassel was trying to climb down to safety.

Steenwyck took him by the collar, pulling him back. "You'll kill us all! You're the one the Horseman wants! Why should we die for you? Get out of the church!"

Others joined Steenwyck, grabbing onto Baltus, dragging him toward the church door.

Ichabod struggled through the crowd, pulling people away. "Stop this! The Horseman cannot enter! It does not matter who he wants—he cannot cross the gate!"

"He's coming back!" a rifleman called from a window. "With a coil of rope!"

Steenwyck pointed a fleshy finger at Baltus. "We have to save ourselves!"

"No! Unhand me!" In desperation, Baltus grabbed Ichabod's pistol.

His captors scattered as Baltus waved the gun around. "Stand off! The next person to lay hands on me will have a bullet!"

Now Dr. Lancaster was pushing his way through the mob. He confronted Steenwyck eye to eye. "Enough have died already! It is time to confess our sins and ask God to forgive our trespasses!"

"Don't be a fool!" Steenwyck shot back. "I warn you, Doctor—"

"What is it that you know, Lancaster?" Baltus demanded.

Steenwyck didn't wait to hear the answer. He ran toward the altar, disappearing into the crowd.

"Your four friends play you false," Dr. Lancaster replied. "We were devilishly possessed by one who—"

In a flash Steenwyck appeared behind him, brandishing a heavy cross.

Before anyone could react, Steenwyck brought the cross down hard, a direct hit to the back of Lancaster's head.

The doctor fell lifelessly to the floor. Baltus lifted his pistol and took careful aim at Steenwyck.

No. It's all happening too fast. It can't be . . .

In the surrounding clamor, few heard Baltus's shot. And no one helped the reverend as he clutched his abdomen and collapsed.

Ichabod watched helplessly. Everything was disintegrating—rules, morality, logic. . . .

He raced toward Katrina. She stood now, facing the church, numb at the sight of the bloody spectacle.

"There is a conspiracy here!" Baltus's voice boomed out. "And I will seek it out!"

With a crash that obliterated all other sound, an iron fence post hurtled through a window.

It spiraled across the room, pointed and sturdy, trailing a long rope. Dirt spat from the bottom, where it had been ripped from the earth. Its path was swift and sure, with a speed that allowed no reaction. It stopped only when it met its target, Baltus Van Tassel.

His body lurched forward as the point emerged through his chest. His eyes, wide and losing focus, scanned the room as if to plead for help. Then he fell to his knees, his body propped up grotesquely by the post.

Ichabod watched, horrified. He was aware of the townspeople running for the corners. He heard their screams. He felt Katrina fainting into his arms. But it was all as if through the thick murk of a dream.

Baltus was the last link. He had found sanctuary. He had avoided the wrath of the conspirators. But the Horseman had found a way. His killing craft could not be stopped.

Numb, Ichabod lowered Katrina gently to the ground. He had to concentrate on her now, protect her. In this madness she would be easily crushed.

As he moved her away from the trampling feet, he caught sight of a ribbon around her neck and a bauble that hung from it.

The crone's bauble.

Ichabod's heart lurched in his chest. What now? What was Katrina doing with this? What connection could she possibly have with the Witch of the Western Woods? Someone in the church must have given it to her.

No matter. He needed to get her to a safe spot.

Gently pulling her to the wall, he spotted a familiar shape hastily drawn in chalk on the flagstones of the altar—a pentagram identical to the one he'd found under his bed.

"The Evil Eye again," Ichabod murmured.

The person who drew it had to be here. Perhaps it was the one who had given Katrina the bauble. Perhaps the bauble marked her in some way.

As he adjusted Katrina's limp body, a small object rolled to the floor from her hand. Ichabod's eyes followed it with mounting disbelief.

It was chalk.

"Oh, God," he murmured. "It was you."

He looked into the motionless, serene face of the only woman he'd ever loved. Katrina—the Horseman's conjurer? It didn't seem conceivable. It couldn't be true. There had to be an explanation.

No. Nothing is logical. Everything is possible. You cannot trust a soul.

He sank to the floor, the pain in his heart obliterating everything around him.

Suddenly the church rang out with terrified shouting.

The fence post rope had grown taut. Baltus's body was flying backward through the church, like a hooked fish being pulled on a line. With a loud crash, he burst through a window.

Ichabod sat up and looked through the gaping hole. Daredevil was galloping away, the rope tied to his saddle pommel, pulling Baltus with him.

With a dull clang, Baltus's mangled body slammed against the fence, held fast by the rope. His head hung back limply through the iron bars.

Ichabod recoiled.

Her own father, a victim of the Horseman—the spirit she herself summoned.

Did she know? How could she have done this?

How?

"Oh, Katrina!" Ichabod moaned, holding her tighter. "Oh, God, forgive her!"

The Headless Horseman circled around and rode back to the fence.

With a swift, sure thrust, he cut off the head of Baltus Van Tassel.

15

KATRINA'S FACE HAD LOST ITS COLOR. IT NEARLY blended in with the bleached whiteness of her bed-sheets. Ichabod sat by her bed, trying to understand what had happened and figure out what to do next.

How could he complete his job? How could he explain what he'd seen? Who would believe Katrina capable of such evil, such slaughter? Such greed? And even if the truth were known, then what? What would happen to Katrina?

It was over now. Lady Van Tassel was dead, and Baltus. No one remained in the line of succession. No one left to kill.

I can't . . . I can't tell a soul.

Ichabod touched his hand to Katrina's face tenderly. He knew it would be his last contact with her forever, and yet he had so much to say. Regret and sadness and bewilderment battled within him, but an explanation for Katrina's actions was emerging from it all. It was a notion he once would have found preposterous, but now he accepted it for lack of anything better.

He whispered it to her, hoping she might hear it in her dreams. "It was an evil spirit possessed you. I pray God it is satisfied now and that you find peace. Good-bye, Katrina. The Evil Eye has done its work. My life is over—spared for a lifetime of horrors in my sleep, waking each day to grief."

Katrina's face remained calm, insensate, as Ichabod left the room.

He still had time to pack and call a coach.

Ichabod left the house at dawn. Young Masbath reluctantly helped him carry his luggage. The boy was sullen, angry that Ichabod was leaving, but Ichabod had made up his mind.

Gathering dry twigs into a circle of rocks at the edge of the lawn, he coaxed a fire to life. Into it he tossed his ledger. He watched as the years of accumulated observation, deduction, and knowledge were consumed by the blaze. Sense and logic had betrayed him in Sleepy Hollow. He had no faith in them anymore.

Reaching into his satchel he pulled out another book, the slim, compact volume that Katrina had given him: *A Compendium of Spells, Charms, and Devices of the Spirit World.*

I told her I had no use for this. Perhaps if I'd read it, I could have prevented some of the carnage.

Behind him, a coach was pulling to a stop. Gunpowder was part of the team, and Ichabod gave him a sad smile.

Ichabod dropped the book back into his satchel. The driver, Van Ripper, helped him load the luggage onto the coach.

Young Masbath stood still, not assisting at all. "But who will look for the truth when you have gone?" he blurted out.

"There is no more truth to be found," Ichabod replied. "That is why I can go and leave this wretched place behind me."

"You think it was Katrina, don't you?"

"That can never be uttered! Never."

Young Masbath glared at him. Ichabod knew he had not answered the question directly, only given the boy an implication and an order, and Young Masbath resented both. "A strange sort of witch," the boy said scornfully, "with a kind and loving heart! How can you think so?"

"I have good reason."

"Then *you* are bewitched—by reason!"

The boy was young, emotional, and principled—good qualities. But Ichabod knew now what Young Masbath would need to learn—that even one's emotions must yield to physical evidence and that certain wounds must stay closed forever.

"I am beaten down with reason," Ichabod said. "It is a hard lesson for a hard world, and you had better learn it, Young Masbath. Villainy wears many masks, and none so dangerous as the mask of virtue. Farewell."

The boy stared back, his eyes defiant yet rimmed with tears. Ichabod knew he had lost the boy's respect, but no matter. In time, even Young Masbath would understand. Turning away, Ichabod climbed into the coach.

As Van Ripper seated himself, Ichabod cast one final glance at the Van Tassel manor. Only one light shone—the light from Katrina's room, on the second floor. He averted his eyes, trying to begin the process of forgetting.

The coach took off with a sudden lurch. As it rolled down the road, Ichabod felt a sharp pain. It started in his gut and traveled in a wave to his head, causing his eyes to well up—all the pent-up frustration and horror and grief finally letting loose. He pounded the side of the coach, trying to blunt the agony.

In his despair, he didn't see Katrina's face pressing against the window, her cheeks streaked with tears.

Ichabod strove to regain his composure. He gazed forward listlessly, swallowing his emotions, as the coach crossed the covered bridge and rolled past the town square. The church was still in a shambles, the window broken, the iron gate mangled.

Soon, Ichabod told himself, these would be fixed. In time the town would prosper again, and this tragedy would recede to legend. Perhaps someday he would pass through on his way north, and not a soul would remember his face.

Near Dr. Lancaster's office they came upon a slow-moving horse pulling a cart. An undertaker was walking alongside, his face lowered, in the practiced grimness of his profession. *Many of these will pass through Sleepy Hollow in the days to come,* Ichabod thought. He looked into the cart as they passed, stealing a glance at the body.

He knew who it was immediately. The head was missing, but one palm was gashed severely.

Lady Van Tassel.

Ichabod stifled a gasp. She had been a kind woman but impossible to fathom. At least Baltus had been spared the grief of her burial.

The cart was leaving the town limits now and also, Ichabod hoped, the last reminder of the awful tragedy. As he settled into the seat, he listened to the cricket chirps wane, replaced by the fresh, hopeful songs of the morning birds.

A sudden clopping of hoofbeats made him turn around. Another rider was approaching fast. It was a woman, her shape quickly becoming familiar— Katrina.

He felt a rush of hope, of happiness, but he knew that feeling was foolhardy. And she was foolhardy if she thought she'd catch him.

Katrina was riding past the undertaker's cart now, slowing down to take a look.

Ichabod turned away. He had seen enough misery. He could not bear to see it again, on the face of the only woman he'd ever loved.

Nonetheless he listened for the resumption of hoofbeats behind them. Part of him held out hope that Katrina would follow.

But the sound never came.

Van Ripper's horses were slow, and the ride even more bumpy than the one from New York. In between bone-jarring potholes, Ichabod had somehow drifted off to sleep. Every dream had been of Katrina.

By midafternoon, he was thirsty and agitated. He reached into his satchel for a bottle of water. His fingers grazed against Katrina's book. Pulling it out, he thought he caught the faint scent of honeysuckle.

He leafed through the book absently until he

reached a page that contained a familiar diagram—a
pentagram, the Evil Eye. The same design Katrina
had drawn twice.

Over the picture was a headline: "For the Protection of a Loved One Against Evil Spirits."

Protection.

Ichabod nearly dropped the book. He stared at the
words in shock. They chided him, mocked him.

The pentagram wasn't a curse at all. It was a
blessing. All his assumptions about the case—all his
assumptions about Katrina—had been wrong.

*She was trying to help me by drawing the symbol under
my bed. She was trying to help herself by drawing it in the
church.*

*Katrina was not the one who summoned the Headless
Horseman. How could I have been so stupid?*

"But then who?" Ichabod muttered. The Hessian
must still be at large, which meant the carnage could
continue. The town was still in danger. Perhaps Katrina was in danger.

He stared at the book, hoping for some indication,
some further clue. His scarred hands flipped through
the pages. Images raced through his mind—the
bizarre events, the beheadings, the enchantments,
the blood and the cauterizations, the unanswered
questions.

*My hands . . . if I can understand them, I can figure
this out, too.*

From the maelstrom of confusion, the answer
arose. Suddenly Ichabod knew. The murderer could
be only one person—a person immune from suspi-
cion.

He slammed the book closed. Looking through it
had helped more than he could have ever hoped.

"Keep it close to your heart," Katrina had said.

Ichabod needed all the magic in the world now. He dropped the book into his breast pocket.

"Van Ripper, turn the coach!" he bellowed. "Take me to Dr. Lancaster!"

The trip felt like an eternity. The sun had set by the time they arrived. Grabbing his satchel, Ichabod ran up the walkway and pounded on the door.

Mrs. Lancaster opened it, peering out with the aid of a lantern. Ichabod snatched it from her and barged inside. "Pardon my intrusion."

Two coffins lay on the floor of the medical room. Ichabod threw the lid off one, revealing the headless body of Baltus Van Tassel.

Wrong one.

He opened the other coffin. Lady Van Tassel's headless corpse lay peacefully, arms folded. He lifted her hand and examined the gash closely, pulling at the stitches.

Yes. It was just as he'd suspected.

"No blood flow, no clotting, no healing," he said. "When this cut was made, this woman was already dead!"

Without saying a further word to Mrs. Lancaster, he picked up his satchel and raced out.

In the Van Tassel house, Katrina sat in the parlor before the dying hearthfire. She had sat there all day since seeing her stepmother's corpse. Her eyes were closed in the mounting darkness; she had no desire to light candles or stoke the fire. As she thought about all that had happened, she asked herself for the millionth time, why.

Father was gone and stepmother and Ichabod. All

in one day. All the love in her life vanquished. Perhaps Ichabod had been right. Perhaps magic was good for nothing.

A creaking floorboard snapped her out of her daze. "Who is there?" she called out.

Into the dim, flickering light stepped a figure dressed in black, someone Katrina had seen every day for years.

Someone she'd never expected to see again.

It can't be!

She jumped to her feet. Her mouth opened but no words came out.

Lady Van Tassel threw back her head and cackled. "Dear stepdaughter, you look as if you've seen a ghost!"

16

SHE'S DEAD.

I saw her corpse.

She couldn't have been in the parlor.

That was a dream.

Katrina stirred, but she was still sleeping. She must have been because she was in a strange place—an imaginary one that was cold, freezing cold.

The familiar outlines of her parlor had given way to a vast room, dark and drafty. Against the wooden walls, a dull light cast strange shadows, dancing among the old equipment and sacks of grain.

The windmill. It was the only place this could be.

Katrina's eyes followed the strange light to its source: a lantern on the cement floor. Near it crouched Lady Van Tassel, leaning over an odd pile of debris that included a small bird's heart, pierced with a roofing nail.

This *was* an odd dream. The real Lady Van Tassel knew nothing of conjuring piles. Of course Katrina did; any student of magic would. They summoned spirits of the dead.

Muttering softly, her dream-image stepmother sprinkled a lock of hair over the pile. Then, using her lantern, she set the pile aflame.

Slowly she lifted something from the bag slung over her shoulder—a skull. And she began chanting: "Rise up once more, my dark avenger, rise up! One more night of beheading! Rise up with your sword, and your mistress of the night will make you whole. A head for a head, my unholy Horseman. Rise, rise, rise from the earth—come forth again through the Tree of the Dead. *Come now for Katrina!*"

A flash of lightning rent the sky.

NO!

Katrina sat up sharply. She felt her head. A lock of hair was missing, snipped off crudely. This was real. Lady Van Tassel was alive.

"Awake at last," Lady Van Tassel said. "Did you think it was all a nasty dream? Alas, no."

Katrina stared at her in disbelief. "My father saw the Horseman kill you."

"He saw the Horseman coming to me with his sword unsheathed. But it is I who govern the Horseman, my dear, and Baltus did not stay to see."

"But—I saw your body, outside Dr. Lancaster's house!"

Lady Van Tassel laughed. "That was the servant girl, Sarah. I always thought her useless, but she turned out useful. Tomorrow I'll totter out of the woods and spin a tale how I found Baltus and Sarah in the act of lust. As I watched, the Horseman was upon them, and off went Sarah's head! I fainted and remember nothing more."

This was not the woman Katrina had known all these years, the stepmother with whom she'd shared a home and a family, trust and love. This was no human being at all.

"Who are you?"

Lady Van Tassel looked levelly into Katrina's eyes. "My family name was Archer."

"The archer . . ." Katrina thought back. The name meant something.

The drawing on the back of the fireplace. In our old cottage.

"I lived with my father and mother and my sister in a gamekeeper's cottage not far from here," Lady Van Tassel went on, her voice darkening, "until, one day, my father died. The landlord, who had received many years of loyal service from my parents, evicted us. No one in this god-fearing town would take us in because my mother was suspected of witchcraft. She was no witch, but I believe she knew much that lies under the surface of life—and she schooled her daughters well while we lived as outcasts in the Western Woods. She died within a year, and my sister and I remained in our refuge, seeing not a soul— until, gathering firewood one day, we crossed the path of the Hessian. He was running from Revolutionary soldiers, seeking a hiding place to mount a surprise attack. My sister ran, but I remained. The

Hessian put his finger to his lips, warning me to be silent. I had no fear. I held up a dry branch and snapped it in two. The sound rang out in the woods like a pistol shot, instantly drawing the soldiers."

Katrina remembered the old legend. It had been thought that the Headless Horseman had stepped on a branch, revealing his own whereabouts.

"I saw his death," Lady Van Tassel said. "And later on, hiding in the woods, I witnessed his burial. From that moment, I offered my soul to Satan if he would raise the Hessian from the dead to avenge me."

"Avenge you?" Katrina asked.

"Against Van Garrett, who evicted my family. Against Baltus Van Tassel, who, with wife and simpering girl child, stole our home."

Katrina was speechless.

How can she accuse us of stealing? Father was hired by Van Garrett as gamekeeper. Van Garrett gave us the cottage. We didn't know a thing about any Archer family.

"I swore I would make myself mistress of all they had!" Lady Van Tassel laughed shrilly. "The easiest part was the first: to enter your house as your mother's sick-nurse and put her body into the grave and my own into the marriage bed."

Katrina cried out. This was sick, inhuman.

"Not quite so easy was to secure my legacy," Lady Van Tassel continued, "but lust delivered Reverend Steenwyck into my power. Fear did the same for the Notary Hardenbrook. The drunken Philipse succumbed for a share of the proceeds. And the doctor's silence I exchanged for my complicity in his adulteries."

Slowly a shadow moved into the light, behind Lady Van Tassel. Katrina saw it peripherally but instantly knew not to look.

It was Young Masbath, holding a large wooden mallet.

"Yes," Katrina said, stalling to give the boy time, "you have everything now."

"No, my dear, *you* do, by virtue of your father's will. But I get everything in the event of your death." Lady Van Tassel snatched the talisman from around Katrina's neck. "This pretty bauble, which I so kindly gave you to wear, has done its work. My sister, by the way, sadly passed away quite recently."

The Witch of the Western Woods. She was the owner of this charm.

Katrina resolutely looked in Lady Van Tassel's eyes, ignoring Young Masbath. "It was the crone you killed," she said. "Your own sister!"

The boy inched closer, preparing to strike.

"She brought it on herself"—suddenly Lady Van Tassel whirled around toward her attacker, cackling loudly—"by helping you and your master!"

Young Masbath shrieked. His mallet dropped to the floor.

"You are just in time to have your head sliced off," Lady Van Tassel said.

A crack of thunder shook the earth. Young Masbath and Katrina ran to each other as Lady Van Tassel looked up to the sky. "The Horseman comes. And tonight, my dear Katrina, he comes for you."

She reached into the conjuring pile and lifted the Horseman's skull. Bringing it level to her face, she let out a chilling, beastlike cry. In the distance, a horse's fierce whinny answered.

Katrina seized up. He was on his way, and she was trapped.

Go. Now. Outrun him.

She leaped to her feet and raced from the windmill with Young Masbath close behind.

"Run!" Lady Van Tassel taunted. "There is no escape!"

In front of the Van Tassel house, Ichabod leaped from the carriage. He had driven the horses himself, leaving Van Ripper behind when the laggard had taken too long during a rest stop.

"Katrina!" he shouted, bounding up the front stairs.

The house was dark, and his only answer was a crack of thunder.

He spun around. Lightning flashed distantly, illuminating a structure on the top of a hill—the old windmill, which was now lit from within.

It shouldn't be lit. Not at this hour. Not in this weather.

Someone was there, and he had an awful feeling he knew who.

He sprinted back to the carriage and spurred the horses on. As they sped across the field, the wind kicked up violently, threatening to blow Ichabod off the carriage.

The Horseman's wind. The Horseman's storm.

He held the reins tight as the horses took the hill. Two shadows were emerging from the windmill now, rushing toward him. When they came into sight, Ichabod's heart leaped.

They were Young Masbath and Katrina—alive.

At the top of the hill, Ichabod pulled the horses to a stop. Taking a lantern, he leaped off and ran toward the two, wrapping them in an embrace. They were shivering and panting with fright, and Ichabod could only murmur, "Thank God!"

His relief was chilled instantly by a piercing laugh from within the windmill. It was like nothing Ichabod had ever heard. It was like the sound of death itself.

A white horse emerged from the open door, carrying Lady Van Tassel. At the same time, an insistent drumming below announced the approach of Daredevil and the Headless Horseman.

"Have you come back to arrest him after all?" screamed Lady Van Tassel.

Ichabod looked behind. The Horseman was thundering up the hill. He would be on them in a second. Trying to escape would be foolish. Staying still would be suicide.

Ichabod pulled Young Masbath and Katrina back toward the windmill. "Quickly!" he shouted.

Lady Van Tassel faced the Horseman, holding the skull up high. "Mind your hat, Constable!" she shrieked.

The windmill entrance was a trapdoor in the floor of a jutting overhang. A ladder extended from it. Young Masbath scurried up first, then Katrina.

Ichabod looked over his shoulder. The Horseman had dismounted and was heading toward him on foot. Ichabod scrambled up the ladder and into the windmill. He pushed the heavy wooden door shut.

A sudden pounding from below made Ichabod fall back. The Horseman was chopping at the door, splitting it up the middle.

"It won't hold!" Young Masbath yelled.

Ichabod ran to the wall, where a large grindstone leaned upright. Young Masbath helped him roll it to the trapdoor, then let it fall.

It landed on the door with a thump just as the Horseman's sword plunged through the center hole.

Young Masbath jumped. The Horseman retracted the sword and began pounding, hacking against the trapdoor with his ax. It wouldn't be long now. Stone and wood wouldn't stop him. Something else would have to.

Ichabod needed a plan of action. He looked around frantically at the windmill's massive center shaft, attached to the rotors by a set of perpendicular cogged gears . . . at the pair of grindstones and the grain bin beneath it . . . at the ladder that led to a high wooden milling platform . . . at the huge sacks of milled grain lying on the platform . . . at the rickety stairs that spiraled upward to the roof . . .

A desperate idea formed.

He grabbed a baling hook. "Get up those stairs," he said to Katrina. "Open the door to the roof and wait."

He handed her his lantern, and she scurried up the stairs with Young Masbath.

Ichabod climbed up the ladder to the platform. There, a wooden lever was locked in position, keeping the windmill gears still. He yanked the lever down. Slowly the rotors began spinning, turning the cogs and the central shaft.

WWHAACK! WHAACK! WHAACK!

The grindstone above the trapdoor was jumping against the Horseman's blows. It was only a matter of seconds now.

"Ichabod!" Katrina called from above.

"Keep climbing! I will follow!" Ichabod shouted. Under his breath he added, "I hope."

The sacks were heavy. Dragging them to the platform took all Ichabod's strength. When they were lined up at the edge, he lifted the baling hook and struck, puncturing each bag one by one.

Grain dust cascaded off the platform, landing on the windmill floor. It billowed up in a cloud, thick and choking.

WWHAACK! WHAACK!

The grindstone fell through the trapdoor, hitting the ground with a thud. The Horseman had chopped away at the edges of the door frame.

Now grain dust was rising to the platform. Soon it would obliterate Ichabod's vision. He looked up to see Young Masbath climbing out the roof door with Katrina.

He'd have to follow them. He eyed the stairs that spiraled along the inner wall of the windmill. He realized at once that the stairs were too far away. The platform was in the center and did not extend to the walls.

To reach the stairs, Ichabod would have to go down to the lower level.

"Behind you!" Katrina called from above.

Ichabod whirled around. Through the mushrooming billows of dust, the Horseman emerged.

No going down now. Ichabod would have to jump for the stairs. He ran to the edge of the platform. Desperately he leaped, reaching with his hands . . . dropping fast . . .

His fingers closed on the outer railing. He clutched tight, pulling himself onto the stairs.

As he began climbing, he coughed out the dry grain dust and blinked it out of his eyes. It seemed to be expanding, displacing the oxygen in the windmill.

From above, Young Masbath and Katrina beckoned to him through the open roof door.

The Horseman was swinging on a chain now, cutting a wind current through the dust cloud. He landed with a heavy thump on the stairs, not far below Ichabod.

Ichabod scrambled to the top. Katrina and Young Masbath pulled him through the door. "Quickly, close it!" Katrina cried out.

"No!" Ichabod replied, taking the lantern from her. "Get to the crest of the roof and be ready to jump."

"Jump?" Young Masbath said. "From up here?"

The Horseman was close. There was no time to argue. Ichabod led the other two out onto the sloping rooftop.

The windmill's rotors swung steadily in front of them, their sailcloth covers snapping in the wind. "Jump for the sails," Ichabod commanded. "Wait till I give the word."

Katrina was stiff with panic. "Ichabod! I can't!"

"Yes, you can, my love—hand in hand." Ichabod inched back to the open roof door. He could see the Horseman's shadow moving up through the grain cloud, dry and thickening. "Be ready . . ."

He held the lantern out into the opening—and dropped it.

"NOW!"

Young Masbath jumped. Ichabod grabbed Katrina and followed. They landed together on one of the windmill rotors. Ichabod held tightly to Katrina as they traveled slowly downward.

He heard the smashing of glass inside—the lantern, hitting the floor.

The windmill shook as the grain dust exploded into flames.

Ichabod, Katrina, and Young Masbath could hold onto the rotors no longer. They tumbled to the ground, landing on the soft earth. Scrambling to their feet, they ran down the hill.

The windmill was a column of fire, spitting chunks of debris. They could feel the heat at their backs as they sped across the field.

They stopped at the edge of the woods. Ichabod's coach was nearby. The horses grazed, eyeing the windmill skittishly. It was crumbling now, falling to the ground in sections of flame.

The Horseman was in there, too, Ichabod thought. *Somewhere.*

"Is he dead?" Young Masbath asked.

"He was dead to begin with," Ichabod replied. "That's the problem."

"Look!" Katrina shouted.

A pile of burning rubble was shifting, moving. Ichabod watched it, his disbelief giving way to abject terror.

Out of the flames, his body intact, arose the Headless Horseman.

17

"COME ON!" ICHABOD SHOUTED.

He ran to the coach and jumped on. Katrina and Young Masbath followed right behind him.

Ichabod grabbed the reins, but he didn't have to

do much. The horses took off, galloping at top speed on the trail toward the woods.

Behind them, Daredevil's whinny pierced the air.

"Where are we going?" Katrina asked.

"Anywhere," Ichabod answered.

"He's right behind!" Young Masbath shouted.

"Make for the church!" Katrina said.

"We'll never reach it!" Ichabod replied.

Young Masbath snatched Ichabod's satchel off the coach floor and thrust it toward him. "Here, sir. You must have something in your bag of tricks."

"Nothing that will help us, I am afraid. Take the reins!"

Young Masbath traded places with him.

Ichabod grabbed Van Ripper's rifle. Giving it to Katrina, he climbed onto the coach roof and began crawling toward the storage box at the rear.

The Horseman was close. Ichabod could smell the decay of his flesh, the burnt material of his uniform. He was coming up alongside the coach, unsheathing his sword.

Ichabod reached down, opened the box, and found what he needed, a handsaw.

"Look out!" Katrina shouted.

Ichabod heard the sword and ducked away. It smashed against the coach, splintering wood.

Close. Too close.

The Horseman was backing away now, switching to the other side of the trail and then beginning his approach again.

Ichabod crawled toward the front of the coach. "Keep him off! Block him!"

Young Masbath guided the horses to the side of

the road, squeezing the Horseman, forcing him to fall back.

The wheels bounced over the rough gutter stones, and Ichabod flew off the roof.

Frantically he reached out. His fingers gripped the frame of the door. He hung off the side, clutching tightly, his shoes scraping the road. Out of the corner of his eye, he saw the handsaw fall, vanishing in the dust.

Katrina reached out. "Take my hand!"

He stretched toward her, trying to clasp her fingers.

With a sudden smack, the door fell open. Ichabod swung away, clinging to the frame. His pistol, jarred loose from its holster, fell to the road.

Branches were hitting his face. The coach was too close to the trees. He had to get away. He lunged for the edge of the coach window and managed to grip it.

He pulled himself inside the coach, tumbling to the floor just as the trunk of a hemlock tore the door off.

As Young Masbath veered the coach to the other side of the road, the Horseman moved with it, drawing nearer.

Katrina gave Ichabod the rifle. He quickly turned it toward the Horseman, trying to steady his aim against the violent jostling.

The Horseman leaned over Daredevil and grabbed onto the back of the coach.

Ichabod fired.

The Horseman's hand was blown to shreds. He let go but continued to grip the coach with his other hand.

Ichabod took aim again.

Then his jaw dropped in awe. The Horseman was grabbing with both hands now, even though one was little more than bone and gristle. He was sliding off Daredevil, climbing onto the coach. Once on board, he stood intact and able, raising his sword.

Ichabod swung the rifle, full force. The Horseman slapped it away, sending Ichabod to the floor.

Suddenly Young Masbath loomed over him, swinging Ichabod's satchel. It hit the Horseman in the chest, catching him off balance.

He stumbled, his arms windmilling, and fell off the coach onto the road.

"It was more useful than you thought!" Young Masbath said.

THWOCCCKK!

The coach smashed against a rock outcropping. It tipped, veering sharply. The front dragged along the road. The horses slowed.

"Hang on!" Ichabod shouted.

They ground to a halt. Ichabod jumped off first, followed by Young Masbath and Katrina. He examined the wheel. It was splintered beyond repair.

"This is not good," Ichabod said.

"We're doomed," Young Masbath added.

On the road behind them, Daredevil screeched, running up to his fallen master.

"We have to get out of the open somehow," Ichabod declared. "Quick, follow me!"

He ran into the woods, up a sharp incline. But he stopped before reaching the top.

Over the crest rode Lady Van Tassel on her white horse. "What, still alive?" she asked Katrina in mock surprise.

In her right hand, she held Ichabod's pistol.

Behind them, Daredevil was closing in fast.

"Run, Katrina!" Ichabod urged.

"Yes, do run. And jump. And skip." Lady Van Tassel aimed the gun carefully at her stepdaughter. "And now let's see a somersault!"

"Run!" Ichabod shouted.

He leaped toward Lady Van Tassel, reaching toward her firing arm. She swiveled slightly, then calmly shot him in the chest.

Ichabod lurched backward and fell.

"No!" Katrina cried.

Young Masbath dropped to his knees. "Oh, God . . . no . . . *no!*"

Lady Van Tassel reached down and yanked Katrina by the hair, dragging her toward the approaching Horseman.

Katrina shrieked, kicking and swinging her arms, but Lady Van Tassel thrust her to the ground. "There she is. Take her, she's yours."

Katrina sprang up and ran back toward Ichabod's body. The Horseman lumbered after her, raising his sword.

Not far away, Ichabod coughed and struggled to his knees.

The shot had hurt, like a blow to the chest. It had been enough to knock him out, but he was alive.

How on earth—

"Sir, you're . . ." Young Masbath said, his voice hushed with awe. "You're not dead."

"Not . . . yet," Ichabod said, not daring to tempt fate.

His attention was drawn by Katrina's shouts. She

was running toward him, with the Horseman close behind. Behind them, Lady Van Tassel gloated.

Ichabod's relief disappeared. The Headless Horseman would not stop until his task was complete, until he killed Katrina. Lady Van Tassel was finally achieving her goal. She had total control over the Horseman. As long as she had what he needed, he was her slave.

That's it.

Ichabod sprang toward Lady Van Tassel. He knocked her off the horse, tackling her to the ground.

Her saddlebag fell, and the Horseman's skull rolled out. Ichabod leaped for it, but Lady Van Tassel grabbed him by the leg, pulling him back.

Suddenly her grip loosened. Ichabod turned to see her sprawled on the grass, unconscious. Young Masbath stood behind her, clutching a tree limb.

"AAAAAGHHH!" Katrina's scream made Ichabod leap up.

The Horseman had caught her. He clutched her hair in one hand and drew back his sword with the other.

Ichabod quickly scooped the skull off the ground and held it out. "Horseman!" he shouted.

The Horseman stopped in midthrust. He angled his body toward Ichabod.

With a mighty heave, Ichabod sent the skull into the air, end over end.

The Horseman instantly dropped Katrina and held out his hands. He caught the skull tenderly, softly.

Katrina raced into Ichabod's arms. The impact sent a bolt of pain through his aching chest, but he didn't care. He held her close and said a prayer of thanks.

The Horseman held out the skull. Slowly he lifted it to his shoulders.

Thunder rocked the countryside and lightning struck the Horseman, surrounding him with a momentary greenish glow. The skull began to transform. In a spark of electricity, flesh assembled itself around the base of the neck. It spread upward, engulfing the bone, filling itself with blood and sinew and muscle and nerve.

Ichabod, Katrina, and Young Masbath staggered backward. This was a miracle. The skull was becoming a head now. Eyes grew, hair sprouted and lengthened to the shoulder—and soon the face of the Hessian was complete.

He was no less frightening as a human. His face was rough, his eyes unyielding as he reached up and touched his jaw. If he was happy, he didn't show it.

Daredevil trotted up to him, whinnying loudly.

The Horseman sheathed his sword, mounted, and rode straight for Ichabod and Katrina.

They clutched each other in terror.

But he rode right past them and kept going toward Lady Van Tassel. Reaching down, the Hessian scooped up the unconscious woman and slung her across Daredevil's back. She bounced gently as he rode off down the hill.

Katrina, Ichabod, and Young Masbath watched, their exhaustion and fear slowly giving way to relief.

With a big smile, Katrina threw her arms around Ichabod's neck. If Ichabod had any doubts about her, they were erased in a long, joyous kiss.

When they broke away from each other, Ichabod called out, "How are you, Young Masbath?"

"Weary, sir," the young man answered with a shy smile.

Ichabod reached out and included him in the embrace. They were partners, all three.

Katrina suddenly drew back. She fingered the bullet hole at Ichabod's chest. "I thought I had lost you."

Ichabod reached into his breast pocket and pulled out a book: *A Compendium of Spells, Charms, and Devices of the Spirit World.*

He had kept it close to his heart.

A bullet was lodged in its midst.

Far from the rejoicing of Ichabod and his companions, the Hessian silently drove his horse along the Indian trail. Ahead, the Tree of the Dead waited.

He was home at last. He could rest now. He could stay here forever.

The lady was awakening now. This was good, the Horseman thought. She would enjoy the journey. After all, she had bought it with her soul.

He gripped her hair and turned her toward him. She opened her eyes—and screamed.

The Hessian drew her face closer to his. He opened his mouth wide, the pointed teeth gleaming in a sudden wash of light.

Daredevil leaped through the air, into the glaring whiteness, toward the opening maw of the tree.

As lightning cracked the night open, the Horseman, his horse, and his lady vanished.

In the sudden darkness that followed, all that was left was the scarred hand of Lady Van Tassel, reaching from the fast-closing gash of the Tree of the Dead, trapped and twitching.

Then it fell limp, blood seeping from the knife wound.

18

YOUNG MASBATH WAS SPEECHLESS. HIS FEET STUM-bled on the paving stones as he looked around at the thriving city and saw more people than he'd seen in a lifetime. "Oh, my!" he murmured for what must have been the hundredth time.

"Cobbled streets!" Katrina exclaimed.

Ichabod chuckled. The snow, falling gently, was covering a multitude of sins. But he had to admit, his city did look enchanting.

It *was* enchanting.

Crime had no exclusive contract here, nor did bad luck, or lost souls. Those could be found anywhere, whether along the weatherbeaten docks or in the quiet country hills, as could many other things—exquisite, wonderful things.

Ichabod smiled at Katrina. "Yes, New York, New York—just in time for the new century. It's the modern age, Katrina!"

"It's always the modern age, Ichabod," Katrina replied. "But the ancient ones endure."

THE LEGEND
OF
SLEEPY HOLLOW

BY WASHINGTON IRVING

A pleasing land of drowsy head it was,
  Of dreams that wave before the half-shut eye;
And of gay castles in the clouds that pass,
  For ever flushing round a summer sky.
                                CASTLE OF INDOLENCE

IN THE BOSOM OF ONE OF THOSE SPACIOUS COVES
which indent the eastern shore of the Hudson, at
that broad expansion of the river denominated by the
ancient Dutch navigators the Tappan Zee, and where
they always prudently shortened sail, and implored
the protection of St. Nicholas when they crossed,
there lies a small market town or rural port, which
by some is called Greensburgh, but which is more
generally and properly known by the name of Tarry
Town. This name was given, we are told, in former
days, by the good housewives of the adjacent country,
from the inveterate propensity of their husbands to
linger about the village tavern on market days. Be
that as it may, I do not vouch for the fact, but merely
advert to it, for the sake of being precise and authentic. Not far from this village, perhaps about two
miles, there is a little valley, or rather lap of land,
among high hills, which is one of the quietest places

in the whole world. A small brook glides through it, with just murmur enough to lull one to repose; and the occasional whistle of a quail or tapping of a woodpecker is almost the only sound that ever breaks in upon the uniform tranquillity.

I recollect that, when a stripling, my first exploit in squirrel shooting was in a grove of tall walnut trees that shades one side of the valley. I had wandered into it at noontime, when all nature is peculiarly quiet, and was startled by the roar of my own gun, as it broke the Sabbath stillness around, and was prolonged and reverberated by the angry echoes. If ever I should wish for a retreat, whither I might steal from the world and its distractions and dream quietly away the remnant of a troubled life, I know of none more promising than this little valley.

From the listless repose of the place, and the peculiar character of its inhabitants, who are descendants from the original Dutch settlers, this sequestered glen has long been known by the name of SLEEPY HOLLOW, and its rustic lads are called the Sleepy Hollow Boys throughout all the neighboring country. A drowsy, dreamy influence seems to hang over the land, and to pervade the very atmosphere. Some say that the place was bewitched by a high German doctor during the early days of the settlement; others, that an old Indian chief, the prophet or wizard of his tribe, held his powwows there before the country was discovered by Master Hendrick Hudson. Certain it is, the place still continues under the sway of some witching power that holds a spell over the minds of the good people, causing them to walk in a continual reverie. They are given to all kinds of marvelous beliefs, are subject to trances and visions, and frequently see strange sights, and hear music and voices in the air. The whole neighborhood abounds with local tales, haunted spots, and twilight superstitions; stars shoot and meteors glare oftener across the valley than in any other part of the country, and the nightmare, with her whole ninefold, seems to make it the favorite scene of her gambols.

The dominant spirit, however, that haunts this enchanted region and seems to be commander-in-chief of all the powers of the air is the apparition of a figure on horseback without a head. It is said by some to be the ghost of a Hessian trooper, whose head had been carried away by a cannon ball, in some nameless battle during the Revolutionary War, and who is ever and anon seen by the country folk, hurrying along in the gloom of night, as if on the wings of the wind. His haunts are not confined to the valley, but extend at times to the adjacent roads, and especially to the vicinity of a church at no great distance. Indeed, certain of the most authentic historians of those parts, who have been careful in collecting and collating the floating facts concerning this specter, allege that the body of the trooper, having been buried in the churchyard, the ghost rides forth to the scene of battle in nightly quest of his head; and that the rushing speed with which he sometimes passes along the Hollow, like a midnight blast, is owing to his being belated, and in a hurry to get back to the churchyard before daybreak.

Such is the general purport of this legendary superstition, which has furnished materials for many a wild story in that region of shadows; and the specter is known, at all the country firesides, by the name of the Headless Horseman of Sleepy Hollow.

It is remarkable that the visionary propensity I have mentioned is not confined to the native inhabitants of the valley, but is unconsciously imbibed by everyone who resides there for a time. However wide awake they may have been before they entered that sleepy region, they are sure, in a little time, to inhale the witching influence of the air, and begin to grow imaginative—to dream dreams and see apparitions.

I mention this peaceful spot with all possible laud; for it is in such little retired Dutch valleys, found here and there embosomed in the great State of New York, that population, manners, and customs remain fixed; while the great torrent of migration and improvement, which is making such incessant changes in other parts of this restless country, sweeps by them unobserved. They are like those little nooks of still water which border a rapid stream, where we may see the straw and bubble riding quietly at anchor, or slowly revolving in their mimic harbor, undisturbed by the rush of the passing current. Though many years have elapsed since I trod the drowsy shades of Sleepy Hollow, yet I question whether I should not still find the same trees and the same families vegetating in its sheltered bosom.

In this by-place of nature there abode, in a remote period of American history, that is to say, some thirty years since, a worthy wight of the name of Ichabod Crane, who sojourned, or, as he expressed it, "tarried," in Sleepy Hollow, for the purpose of instructing the children of the vicinity. He was a native of Connecticut, a State which supplies the Union with pioneers for the mind as well as for the forest, and sends forth yearly its legions of frontier woodsmen and country schoolmasters. The cognomen of Crane was not inapplicable to his person. He was tall, but exceedingly lank, with narrow shoulders, long arms and legs, hands that dangled a mile out of his sleeves, feet that might have served for shovels, and his whole frame most loosely hung together. His head was small, and flat at top, with huge ears, large green glassy eyes, and a long snipe nose, so that it looked like a weathercock, perched upon his spindle neck, to tell which way the wind blew. To see him striding along the profile of a hill on a windy day, with his clothes bagging and fluttering about him, one might have mistaken him for the genius of famine descending upon the earth, or some scarecrow eloped from a cornfield.

His schoolhouse was a low building of one large room, rudely constructed of logs, the windows partly glazed, and partly patched with leaves of old copybooks. It was most ingeniously secured at vacant hours by a withe twisted in the handle of the door and stakes set against the window shutters, so that, though a thief might get in with perfect ease, he would find some embarrassment in getting out; an idea most probably borrowed by the architect, Yost Van Houten, from the mystery of an eel pot. The schoolhouse stood in a rather lonely but pleasant situation, just at the foot of a woody hill, with a brook running close by, and a formidable birch tree growing at one end of it. From hence the low murmur of his pupils' voices, conning over their lessons, might be heard in a drowsy summer's day, like the hum of a beehive, interrupted now and then by the authoritative voice of the master, in the tone of menace or command, or, peradventure, by the appalling sound of the birch, as he urged some tardy loiterer along the flowery path of knowledge. Truth to say, he was a conscientious man, and ever bore in mind the golden maxim, "Spare the rod and spoil the child." Ichabod Crane's scholars certainly were not spoiled.

I would not have it imagined, however, that he was one of those cruel potentates of the school who joy in the smart of their subjects; on the contrary, he administered justice with discrimination rather than severity, taking the burthen off the backs of the weak, and laying it on those of the strong. Your mere puny stripling that winced at the least flourish of the rod was passed by with indulgence; but the claims of justice were satisfied by inflicting a double portion on some little, tough, wrong-headed, broad-skirted Dutch urchin, who sulked and swelled and grew dogged and sullen beneath the birch. All this he called "doing his duty by their parents"; and he never inflicted a chastisement without following it by the assurance, so consolatory to the smarting urchin, that "he would remember it, and thank him for it the longest day he had to live."

When school hours were over, he was even the companion and playmate of the larger boys; and on holiday afternoons would convoy some of the smaller ones home, who happened to have pretty sisters, or good housewives for mothers, noted for the comforts of the cupboard. Indeed it behooved him to keep on good terms with his pupils. The revenue arising from his school was small, and would have been scarcely sufficient to furnish him with daily bread, for he was a huge feeder, and though lank, had the dilating powers of an anaconda; but to help out his mainte-nance, he was, according to country custom in those parts, boarded and lodged at the houses of the farm-

ers whose children he instructed. With these he lived
successively a week at a time; thus going the rounds
of the neighborhood, with all his worldly effects tied
up in a cotton handkerchief.

That all this might not be too onerous on the
purses of his rustic patrons, who are apt to consider
the costs of schooling a grievous burden and schoolmasters as mere drones, he had various ways of ren-
dering himself both useful and agreeable. He assisted
the farmers occasionally in the lighter labors of their
farms, helped to make hay, mended the fences, took
the horses to water, drove the cows from pasture, and
cut wood for the winter fire. He laid aside, too, all
the dominant dignity and absolute sway with which
he lorded it in his little empire, the school, and became wonderfully gentle and ingratiating. He found
favor in the eyes of the mothers by petting the children, particularly the youngest; and like the lion
bold, which whilom so magnanimously the lamb did
hold, he would sit with a child on one knee, and rock
a cradle with his foot for whole hours together.

In addition to his other vocations, he was the
singing master of the neighborhood, and picked up
many bright shillings by instructing the young folks
in psalmody. It was a matter of no little vanity to
him, on Sundays, to take his station in front of the
church gallery, with a band of chosen singers; where,
in his own mind, he completely carried away the
palm from the parson. Certain it is, his voice resounded far above all the rest of the congregation;
and there are peculiar quavers still to be heard in
that church, and which may even be heard half a
mile off, quite to the opposite side of the millpond,
on a still Sunday morning, which are said to be le-

gitimately descended from the nose of Ichabod
Crane. Thus, by diverse little makeshifts in that in-
genious way which is commonly denominated "by
hook and by crook," the worthy pedagogue got on
tolerably enough, and was thought, by all who understood nothing of the labor of headwork, to have a
wonderfully easy life of it.

The schoolmaster is generally a man of some importance in the female circle of a rural neighborhood,
being considered a kind of idle gentlemanlike person-
age, of vastly superior taste and accomplishments to
the rough country swains, and, indeed, inferior in
learning only to the parson. His appearance, therefore, is apt to occasion some little stir at the tea table
of a farmhouse, and the addition of a supernumerary
dish of cakes or sweetmeats, or, peradventure, the pa-
rade of a silver teapot. Our man of letters, therefore,
was peculiarly happy in the smiles of all the country
damsels. How he would figure among them in the
churchyard, between services on Sundays! gathering
grapes for them from the wild vines that overrun the
surrounding trees, reciting for their amusement all
the epitaphs on the tombstones, or sauntering, with a
whole bevy of them, along the banks of the adjacent
millpond, while the more bashful country bumpkins
hung sheepishly back, envying his superior elegance
and address.

From his half-itinerant life, also, he was a kind of
traveling gazette, carrying the whole budget of local
gossip from house to house, so that his appearance
was always greeted with satisfaction. He was, moreover, esteemed by the women as a man of his great
erudition, for he had read several books quite
through, and was a perfect master of Cotton Math-

er's *History of New England Witchcraft,* in which, by the way, he most firmly and potently believed.

He was, in fact, an odd mixture of small shrewdness and simple credulity. His appetite for the marvelous, and his powers of digesting it, were equally extraordinary; and both had been increased by his residence in this spellbound region. No tale was too gross or monstrous for his capacious swallow. It was often his delight, after his school was dismissed in the afternoon, to stretch himself on the rich bed of clover, bordering the little brook that whimpered by his schoolhouse, and there con over old Mather's direful tales, until the gathering dusk of the evening made the printed page a mere mist before his eyes. Then, as he wended his way, by swamp and stream and awful woodland, to the farmhouse where he happened to be quartered, every sound of nature, at that witching hour, fluttered his excited imagination: the moan of the whippoorwill* from the hillside; the boding cry of the tree toad, that harbinger of storm; the dreary hooting of the screech owl, or the sudden rustling in the thicket of birds frightened from their roost. The fireflies, too, which sparkled most vividly in the darkest places, now and then startled him, as one of uncommon brightness would stream across his path; and if, by chance, a huge blockhead of a beetle came winging his blundering flight against him, the poor varlet was ready to give up the ghost, with the idea that he was struck with a witch's token. His only resource on such occasions, either to drown thought or drive away evil spirits, was to sing psalm

---

*The whippoorwill is a bird which is only heard at night. It receives its name from its note, which is thought to resemble those words.

tunes; and the good people of Sleepy Hollow, as they sat by their doors of an evening, were often filled with awe, at hearing his nasal melody, "in linked sweetness long drawn out," floating from the distant hill or along the dusky road.

Another of his sources of fearful pleasure was to pass long winter evenings with the old Dutch wives as they sat spinning by the fire, with a row of apples roasting and spluttering along the hearth, and listen to their marvelous tales of ghosts and goblins, and haunted fields, and haunted brooks, and haunted bridges, and haunted houses, and particularly of the headless horseman, or galloping Hessian of the Hollow, as they sometimes called him. He would delight them equally by his anecdotes of witchcraft, and of the direful omens and portentous sights and sounds in the air, which prevailed in the earlier times of Connecticut; and would frighten them woefully with speculations upon comets and shooting stars, and with the alarming fact that the world did absolutely turn around, and that they were half the time topsy-turvy!

But if there was a pleasure in all this, while snugly cuddling in the chimney corner of a chamber that was all of a ruddy glow from the crackling wood fire, and where, of course, no specter dared to show his face, it was dearly purchased by the terrors of his subsequent walk homewards. What fearful shapes and shadows beset his path amidst the dim and ghastly glare of a snowy night! With what wistful look did he eye every trembling ray of light streaming across the waste fields from some distant window! How often was he appalled by some shrub covered with snow, which, like a sheeted specter, beset his very path! How often did he shrink with curdling awe at the sound of his own steps on the frosty crust beneath his feet; and dread to look over his shoulder, lest he should behold some uncouth being tramping close behind him! And how often was he thrown into complete dismay by some rushing blast, howling among the trees, in the idea that it was the Galloping Hessian on one of his nightly scourings!

All these, however, were mere terrors of the night, phantoms of the mind that walk in darkness; and though he had seen many specters in his time, and been more than once beset by Satan in diverse shapes, in his lonely perambulations, yet daylight put an end to all these evils, and he would have passed a pleasant life of it, in despite of the devil and all his works, if his path had not been crossed by a being that causes more perplexity to mortal man than ghosts, goblins, and the whole race of witches put together, and that was—a woman.

Among the musical disciples who assembled, one evening in each week, to receive his instructions in psalmody, was Katrina Van Tassel, the daughter and only child of a substantial Dutch farmer. She was a blooming lass of fresh eighteen, plump as a partridge, ripe and melting and rosy-cheeked as one of her father's peaches, and universally famed not merely for her beauty, but her vast expectations. She was withal a little of a coquette, as might be perceived even in her dress, which was a mixture of ancient and modern fashions, as most suited to set off her charms. She wore the ornaments of pure yellow gold, which her great-great-grandmother had brought over from Saardam; the tempting stomacher of the olden time;

and withal a provokingly short petticoat, to display the prettiest foot and ankle in the country around.

Ichabod Crane had a soft and foolish heart toward the sex; and it is not to be wondered at that so tempting a morsel soon found favor in his eyes, more especially after he had visited her in her paternal mansion. Old Baltus Van Tassel was a perfect picture of a thriving, contented, liberal-hearted farmer. He seldom, it is true, sent either his eyes or his thoughts beyond the boundaries of his own farm; but within those everything was snug, happy, and well-conditioned. He was satisfied with his wealth, but not proud of it; and piqued himself upon the hearty abundance, rather than the style in which he lived. His stronghold was situated on the banks of the Hudson, in one of those green, sheltered, fertile nooks, in which the Dutch farmers are so fond of nestling. A great elm tree spread its broad branches over it, at the foot of which bubbled up a spring of the softest and sweetest water, in a little well, formed of a barrel, and then stole sparkling away through the grass, to a neighboring brook that bubbled along among alders and dwarf willows. Hard by the farmhouse was a vast barn that might have served for a church; every window and crevice of which seemed bursting forth with the treasures of the farm; the flail was busily resounding within it from morning to night; swallows and martins skimmed twittering about the eaves; and rows of pigeons, some with one eye turned up, as if watching the weather, some with their heads' under their wings, or buried in their bosoms, and others swelling, and cooing, and bowing about their dames, were enjoying the sunshine on the roof. Sleek unwieldy porkers were grunting in the repose and abundance of their pens; whence sallied forth, now and then, troops of sucking pigs, as if to snuff the air. A stately squadron of snowy geese were riding in an adjoining pond, convoying whole fleets of ducks; regiments of turkeys were gobbling through the farm-yard, and guinea fowls fretting about it, like ill-tempered housewives, with their peevish discontented cry. Before the barn door strutted the gallant cock, that pattern of a husband, a warrior, and a fine gentleman, clapping his burnished wings and crow-ing in the pride and gladness of his heart—sometimes tearing up the earth with his feet, and then generously calling his ever-hungry family of wives and children to enjoy the rich morsel which he had discovered.

The pedagogue's mouth watered as he looked upon this sumptuous promise of luxurious winter fare. In his devouring mind's eye he pictured to himself every roasting pig running about with a pudding in his belly and an apple in his mouth; the pigeons were snugly put to bed in a comfortable pie, and tucked in with a coverlet of crust; the geese were swimming in their own gravy; and the ducks pairing cozily in dishes, like snug married couples, with a decent competency of onion sauce. In the porkers he saw carved out the future sleek side of bacon, and juicy relishing ham; not a turkey but he beheld daintily trussed up, with its gizzard under its wing, and, peradventure, a necklace of savory sausages; and even bright chanticleer himself lay sprawling on his back, in a sidedish, with uplifted claws, as if craving that quarter which his chivalrous spirit disdained to ask while living.

As the enraptured Ichabod fancied all this, and as

he rolled his great green eyes over the fat meadow lands, the rich fields of wheat, of rye, of buckwheat, and Indian corn, and the orchards burthened with ruddy fruit, which surrounded the warm tenement of Van Tassel, his heart yearned after the damsel who was to inherit these domains, and his imagination expanded with the idea how they might be readily turned into cash, and the money invested in immense tracts of wild land, and shingle palaces in the wilderness. Nay, his busy fancy already realized his hopes, and presented to him the blooming Katrina, with a whole family of children, mounted on the top of a wagon loaded with household trumpery, with pots and kettles dangling beneath; and he beheld himself bestriding a pacing mare, with a colt at her heels, setting out for Kentucky, Tennessee, or the Lord knows where.

When he entered the house the conquest of his heart was complete. It was one of those spacious farmhouses, with high-ridged, but lowly sloping roofs, built in the style handed down from the first Dutch settlers, the low projecting eaves forming a piazza along the front, capable of being closed up in bad weather. Under this were hung flails, harness, various utensils of husbandry, and nets for fishing in the neighboring river. Benches were built along the sides for summer use; and a great spinning wheel at one end, and a churn at the other, showed the various uses to which this important porch might be devoted. From this piazza the wondering Ichabod entered the hall, which formed the center of the mansion and the place of usual residence. Here, rows of resplendent pewter, ranged on a long dresser, dazzled his eyes. In one corner stood a huge bag of wool ready to be spun; in another a quantity of linsey-woolsey just from the loom; ears of Indian corn and strings of dried apples and peaches hung in gay festoons along the walls, mingled with the gaud of red peppers; and a door left ajar gave him a peep into the best parlor, where the claw-footed chairs and dark mahogany tables shone like mirrors; andirons, with their accompanying shovel and tongs, glistened from their covert of asparagus tops; mock oranges and conch shells decorated the mantelpiece; strings of various colored birds' eggs were suspended above it; a great ostrich egg was hung from the center of the room, and a corner cupboard, knowingly left open, displayed immense treasures of old silver and well-mended china.

From the moment Ichabod laid his eyes upon these regions of delight, the peace of his mind was at an end, and his only study was how to gain the affections of the peerless daughter of Van Tassel. In this enterprise, however, he had more real difficulties than generally fell to the lot of a knight-errant of yore, who seldom had anything but giants, enchanters, fiery dragons, and such like easily conquered adversaries to contend with; and had to make his way merely through gates of iron and brass, and walls of adamant, to the castle keep, where the lady of his heart was confined; all which he achieved as easily as a man would carve his way to the center of a Christmas pie; and then the lady gave him her hand as a matter of course. Ichabod, on the contrary, had to win his way to the heart of a country coquette, beset with a labyrinth of whims and caprices, which were forever presenting new difficulties and impediments; and he had to encounter a host of fearful adversaries of real flesh and blood, the numerous rustic admirers, who beset every portal to her heart, keeping a watchful and angry eye upon each other, but ready to fly out in the common cause against any new competitor.

Among these the most formidable was a burly, roaring, roystering blade, of the name of Abraham, or, according to the Dutch abbreviation, Brom Van Brunt, the hero of the country round, which rang with his feats of strength and hardihood. He was broad-shouldered and double-jointed, with short curly black hair, and a bluff but not unpleasant countenance, having a mingled air of fun and arrogance. From his Herculean frame and great powers of limb, he had received the nickname of BROM BONES, by which he was universally known. He was famed for great knowledge and skill in horsemanship, being as dexterous on horseback as a Tartar. He was foremost at all races and cockfights; and, with the ascendency which bodily strength acquires in rustic life, was the umpire in all disputes, setting his hat on one side and giving his decisions with an air and tone admitting of no gainsay or appeal. He was always ready for either a fight or a frolic; but had more mischief than ill will in his composition, and, with all his overbearing roughness, there was a strong dash of waggish good humor at bottom. He had three or four boon companions, who regarded him as their model and at the head of whom he scoured the country, attending every scene of feud or merriment for miles around. In cold weather he was distinguished by a fur cap, surmounted with a flaunting fox's tail; and when the folks at a country gathering descried this well-known crest at a distance, whisking about among a squad of hard riders, they always stood by for a squall. Sometimes his crew would be heard dashing along past the farmhouses at midnight, with whoop and halloo, like a troop of Don Cossacks; and the old dames, startled out of their sleep, would listen for a moment till the hurry-scurry had clattered by, and then exclaim, "Ay, there goes Brom Bones and his gang!" The neighbors looked upon him with a mixture of awe, admiration, and good will; and when any madcap prank or rustic brawl occurred in the vicinity, always shook their heads and warranted Brom Bones was at the bottom of it.

This rantipole hero had for some time singled out the blooming Katrina for the object of his uncouth gallantries, and though his amorous toyings were something like the gentle caresses and endearments of a bear, yet it was whispered that she did not altogether discourage his hopes. Certain it is, his advances were signals for rival candidates to retire, who felt no inclination to cross a lion in his amours; insomuch, that when his horse was seen tied to Van Tassel's paling, on a Sunday night, a sure sign that his master was courting, or, as it is termed, "sparking," within, all other suitors passed by in despair, and carried the war into other quarters.

Such was the formidable rival with whom Ichabod Crane had to contend, and, considering all things, a stouter man than he would have shrunk from the competition, and a wiser man would have despaired. He had, however, a happy mixture of pliability and perseverance in his nature; he was in form and spirit like a supple jack—yielding, but tough; though he bent, he never broke; and though he bowed beneath the slightest pressure, yet, the moment it was away—jerk! he was as erect, and carried his head as high as ever.

To have taken the field openly against his rival would have been madness, for he was not a man to be thwarted in his amours, any more than that stormy lover Achilles. Ichabod, therefore, made his advances in a quiet and gently insinuating manner. Under cover of his character of singing master, he made frequent visits to the farmhouse; not that he had anything to apprehend from the meddlesome interference of parents, which is so often a stumbling block in the path of lovers. Balt Van Tassel was an easy indulgent soul; he loved his daughter better even than his pipe, and, like a reasonable man and an excellent father, let her have her way in everything. His notable little wife, too, had enough to do to attend to her housekeeping and manage her poultry; for, as she sagely observed, ducks and geese are foolish things, and must be looked after, but girls can take care of themselves. Thus while the busy dame bustled about the house, or plied her spinning wheel at one end of the piazza, honest Balt would sit smoking his evening pipe at the other, watching the achievements of a little wooden warrior, who, armed with a sword in each hand, was most valiantly fighting the wind on the pinnacle of the barn. In the meantime, Ichabod would carry on his suit with the daughter by the side of the spring under the great elm, or sauntering along in the twilight, that hour so favorable to the lover's eloquence.

I profess not to know how women's hearts are wooed and won. To me they have always been matters of riddle and admiration. Some seem to have but one vulnerable point, or door of access, while others have a thousand avenues, and may be captured in a thousand different ways. It is a great triumph of skill to gain the former, but a still greater proof of generalship to maintain possession of the latter, for the man must battle for his fortress at every door and window. He who wins a thousand common hearts is therefore entitled to some renown; but he who keeps undisputed sway over the heart of a coquette is indeed a hero. Certain it is, this was not the case with the redoubtable Brom Bones; and from the moment Ichabod Crane made his advances, the interests of the former evidently declined; his horse was no longer seen tied at the palings on Sunday nights, and a deadly feud gradually arose between him and the preceptor of Sleepy Hollow.

Brom, who had a degree of rough chivalry in his nature, would fain have carried matters to open warfare, and have settled their pretensions to the lady according to the mode of those most concise and simple reasoners, the knights-errant of yore—by single combat; but Ichabod was too conscious of the superior might of his adversary to enter the lists against him. He had overheard a boast of Bones that he would "double the schoolmaster up, and lay him on a shelf of his own schoolhouse," and he was too wary to give him an opportunity. There was something extremely provoking in this obstinately pacific system; it left Brom no alternative but to draw upon the funds of rustic waggery in his disposition, and to play off boorish practical jokes upon his rival. Ichabod became the object of whimsical persecution to Bones and his gang of rough riders. They harried his hitherto peaceful domains; smoked out his singing school by stopping up the chimney; broke into the schoolhouse at night, in spite of its formidable fastenings of withe and window stakes, and turned everything topsy-turvy, so that the poor schoolmaster began to think all the witches in the country held their meetings there. But what was still more annoying, Brom took all opportunities of turning him into ridicule in presence of his mistress, and had a scoundrel dog whom he taught to whine in the most ludicrous manner, and introduced as a rival of Ichabod's to instruct her in psalmody.

In this way matters went on for some time, without producing any material effect on the relative situation of the contending powers. On a fine autumnal afternoon, Ichabod, in pensive mood, sat enthroned on the lofty stool whence he usually watched all the concerns of his little literary realm. In his hand he swayed a ferule, that scepter of despotic power; the birch of justice reposed on three nails, behind the throne, a constant terror to evil-doers; while on the desk before him might be seen sundry contraband articles and prohibited weapons, detected upon the persons of idle urchins, such as half-munched apples, popguns, whirligigs, fly cages, and whole legions of rampant little paper gamecocks. Apparently there had been some appalling act of justice recently inflicted, for his scholars were all busily intent upon their books, or slyly whispering behind them with one eye kept upon the master; and a kind of buzzing stillness reigned throughout the schoolroom. It was suddenly interrupted by the appearance of a Negro, in tow-cloth jacket and trousers, a round-crowned fragment of a hat, like the cap of Mercury, and mounted on the back of a ragged, wild, half-broken colt, which he managed with a rope by way of halter. He came clattering up to the school door with an invitation to Ichabod to attend a merrymaking or "quilting frolic" to be held that evening at Mynheer Van Tassel's; and having delivered his message with that air of importance and effort at fine language which a Negro is apt to display on petty embassies of the kind, he dashed over the brook and was seen scampering away up the hollow, full of the importance and hurry of his mission.

All was now bustle and hubbub in the late quiet schoolroom. The scholars were hurried through their lessons, without stopping at trifles; those who were nimble skipped over half with impunity, and those who were tardy had a smart application now and then in the rear to quicken their speed or help them over a tall word. Books were flung aside without being put away on the shelves, ink-stands were overturned, benches thrown down, and the whole school was turned loose an hour before the usual time, bursting forth like a legion of young imps, yelping and racketing about the green, in joy at their early emancipation.

The gallant Ichabod now spent at least an extra half hour at his toilet, brushing and furbishing up his best and indeed only suit of rusty black, and arranging his looks by a bit of broken looking glass that hung up in the schoolhouse. That he might make his appearance before his mistress in the true style of a cavalier, he borrowed a horse from the farmer with whom he was domiciliated, a choleric old Dutchman of the name of Hans Van Ripper, and, thus gallantly mounted, issued forth, like a knight-errant in quest of adventures. But it is meet I should, in the true spirit of romantic story, give some account of the looks and equipments of my hero and his steed. The animal he bestrode was a broken-down plow horse

that had outlived almost everything but his vicious-
ness. He was gaunt and shagged, with a ewe neck
and a head like a hammer; his rusty mane and tail
were tangled and knotted with burrs; one eye had
lost its pupil and was glaring and spectral, but the
other had the gleam of a genuine devil in it. Still he
must have had fire and mettle in his day, if we may
judge from the name he bore of Gunpowder. He had,
in fact, been a favorite steed of his master's, the choleric Van Ripper, who was a furious rider, and had in-
fused, very probably, some of his own spirit into the
animal, for, old and broken-down as he looked, there
was more of the lurking devil in him than in any
young filly in the country.

Ichabod was a suitable figure for such a steed. He
rode with short stirrups, which brought his knees
nearly up to the pommel of the saddle; his sharp el-
bows stuck out like grasshoppers'; he carried his
whip perpendicularly in his hand, like a scepter, and,
as his horse jogged on, the motion of his arms was
not unlike the flapping of a pair of wings. A small
wool hat rested on the top of his nose, for so his
scanty strip of forehead might be called; and the
skirts of his black coat fluttered out almost to the
horse's tail. Such was the appearance of Ichabod and
his steed, as they shambled out of the gate of Hans
Van Ripper, and it was altogether such an apparition
as is seldom to be met with in broad daylight.

It was, as I have said, a fine autumnal day, the sky
was clear and serene, and nature wore that rich and
golden livery which we always associate with the idea
of abundance. The forests had put on their sober
brown and yellow, while some trees of the tenderer
kind had been nipped by the frosts into brilliant dyes

of orange, purple, and scarlet. Streaming files of wild ducks began to make their appearance high in the air; the bark of the squirrel might be heard from the groves of beech and hickory nuts, and the pensive whistle of the quail at intervals from the neighboring stubble field.

The small birds were taking their farewell banquets. In the fullness of their revelry, they fluttered, chirping and frolicking, from bush to bush, and tree to tree, capricious from the very profusion and variety around them. There was the honest cock robin, the favorite game of stripling sportsmen, with its loud querulous note; and the twittering blackbirds flying in sable clouds; and the golden-winged woodpecker, with his crimson crest, his broad black gorget, and splendid plumage; and the cedar bird, with its red-tipped wings and yellow-tipped tail, and its little monteiro cap of feathers; and the blue jay, that noisy coxcomb, in his gay light-blue coat and white underclothes; screaming and chattering, nodding and bobbing and bowing, and pretending to be on good terms with every songster of the grove.

As Ichabod jogged slowly on his way, his eye, ever open to every symptom of culinary abundance, ranged with delight over the treasures of jolly autumn. On all sides he beheld vast store of apples, some hanging in oppressive opulence on the trees, some gathered into baskets and barrels for the market, others heaped up in rich piles for the cider press. Farther on he beheld great fields of Indian corn, with its golden ears peeping from their leafy coverts and holding out the promise of cakes and hasty pudding; and the yellow pumpkins lying beneath them, turning up their fair round bellies to the sun, and giving

ample prospects of the most luxurious of pies; and
anon he passed the fragrant buckwheat fields, breath-
ing the odor of the beehive, and as he beheld them,
soft anticipations stole over his mind of dainty slap-
jacks, well buttered and garnished with honey or
treacle, by the delicate little dimpled hand of Katrina
Van Tassel.

Thus feeding his mind with many sweet thoughts
and "sugared suppositions," he journeyed along the
sides of a range of hills which look out upon some of
the goodliest scenes of the mighty Hudson. The sun
gradually wheeled his broad disk down into the west.
The wide bosom of the Tappan Zee lay motionless
and glassy, excepting that here and there a gentle un-
dulation waved and prolonged the blue shadow of
the distant mountain. A few amber clouds floated in
the sky, without a breath of air to move them. The
horizon was of a fine golden tint, changing gradually
into a pure apple green, and from that into the deep
blue of the mid-heaven. A slanting ray lingered on
the woody crests of the precipices that overhung
some parts of the river, giving greater depth to the
dark-gray and purple of their rocky sides. A sloop
was loitering in the distance, dropping slowly down
with the tide, her sail hanging uselessly against the
mast; and as the reflection of the sky gleamed along
the still water, it seemed as if the vessel was suspended in the air.

It was toward evening that Ichabod arrived at the
castle of the Heer Van Tassel, which he found
thronged with the pride and flower of the adjacent
country. Old farmers, a spare leathern-faced race, in
homespun coats and breeches, blue stockings, huge
shoes, and magnificent pewter buckles. Their brisk

withered little dames, in close-crimped caps, long-waisted short gowns, homespun petticoats, with scissors and pincushions and gay calico pockets hanging on the outside. Buxom lasses, almost as antiquated as their mothers, excepting where a straw hat, a fine ribbon, or perhaps a white frock gave symptoms of city innovation. The sons, in short square-skirted coats with rows of stupendous brass buttons, and their hair generally queued in the fashion of the times, especially if they could procure an eel skin for the purpose, it being esteemed throughout the country as a potent nourisher and strengthener of the hair.

Brom Bones, however, was the hero of the scene, having come to the gathering on his favorite steed Daredevil, a creature, like himself, full of mettle and mischief, and which no one but himself could manage. He was, in fact, noted for preferring vicious animals, given to all kinds of tricks, which kept the rider in constant risk of his neck, for he held a tractable well-broken horse as unworthy of a lad of spirit.

Fain would I pause to dwell upon the world of charms that burst upon the enraptured gaze of my hero as he entered the state parlor of Van Tassel's mansion. Not those of the bevy of buxom lasses, with their luxurious display of red and white, but the ample charms of a genuine Dutch country tea table, in the sumptuous time of autumn. Such heaped-up platters of cakes of various and almost indescribable kinds, known only to experienced Dutch housewives! There was the doughty doughnut, the tenderer oly koek, and the crisp and crumbling cruller; sweet cakes and shortcakes, ginger cakes and honey cakes, and the whole family of cakes. And then there were apple pies and peach pies and pumpkin pies; besides slices of ham and smoked beef; and moreover delectable dishes of preserved plums, and peaches, and pears, and quinces; not to mention broiled shad and roasted chickens; together with bowls of milk and cream, all mingled higgledy-piggledy, pretty much as I have enumerated them, with the motherly teapot sending up its clouds of vapor from the midst—Heaven bless the mark! I want breath and time to discuss this banquet as it deserves, and am too eager to get on with my story. Happily, Ichabod Crane was not in so great a hurry as his historian, but did ample justice to every dainty.

He was a kind and thankful creature whose heart dilated in proportion as his skin was filled with good cheer, and whose spirits rose with eating as some men's do with drink. He could not help, too, rolling his large eyes around him as he ate, and chuckling with the possibility that he might one day be lord of all this scene of almost unimaginable luxury and splendor. Then, he thought, how soon he'd turn his back upon the old schoolhouse; snap his fingers in the face of Hans Van Ripper, and every other niggardly patron, and kick any itinerant pedagogue out of doors that should dare to call him comrade!

Old Baltus Van Tassel moved about among his guests with a face dilated with content and good humor, round and jolly as the harvest moon. His hospitable attentions were brief, but expressive, being confined to a shake of the hand, a slap on the shoulder, a loud laugh, and a pressing invitation to "fall to, and help themselves."

And now the sound of the music from the common room, or hall, summoned to the dance. The musician was an old gray-headed Negro, who had been the itinerant orchestra of the neighborhood for more than half a century. His instrument was as old and battered as himself. The greater part of the time he scraped on two or three strings, accompanying every movement of the bow with a motion of the head; bowing almost to the ground and stamping with his foot whenever a fresh couple were to start.

Ichabod prided himself upon his dancing as much as upon his vocal powers. Not a limb, not a fiber about him was idle; and to have seen his loosely hung frame in full motion, and clattering about the room, you would have thought Saint Vitus himself, that blessed patron of the dance, was figuring before you in person. He was the admiration of all the Negroes, who, having gathered, of all ages and sizes, from the farm and the neighborhood, stood forming a pyramid of shining black faces at every door and window, gazing with delight at the scene, rolling their white eyeballs, and showing grinning rows of ivory from ear to ear. How could the flogger of urchins be otherwise than animated and joyous? The lady of his heart was his partner in the dance, and smiling graciously in reply to all his amorous oglings, while Brom Bones, sorely smitten with love and jealousy, sat brooding by himself in one corner.

When the dance was at an end, Ichabod was attracted to a knot of the sager folks, who, with old Van Tassel, sat smoking at one end of the piazza, gossiping over former times, and drawing out long stories about the war.

This neighborhood, at the time of which I am speaking, was one of those highly favored places which abound with chronicle and great men. The British and American line had run near it during the war; it had, therefore, been the scene of marauding, and infested with refugees, cowboys, and all kinds of border chivalry. Just sufficient time had elapsed to enable each storyteller to dress up his tale with a little becoming fiction, and, in the indistinctness of his recollection, to make himself the hero of every exploit.

There was the story of Doffue Martling, a large blue-bearded Dutchman, who had nearly taken a British frigate with an old iron nine-pounder from a mud breastwork, only that his gun burst at the sixth discharge. And there was an old gentleman who shall be nameless, being too rich a mynheer to be lightly mentioned, who, in the Battle of White Plains, being an excellent master of defense, parried a musket ball with a small sword, insomuch that he absolutely felt it whiz around the blade and glance off at the hilt, in proof of which he was ready at any time to show the sword, with the hilt a little bent. There were several more that had been equally great in the field, not one of whom but was persuaded that he had a considerable hand in bringing the war to a happy termination.

But all these were nothing to the tales of ghosts and apparitions that succeeded. The neighborhood is rich in legendary treasures of the kind. Local tales and superstitions thrive best in these sheltered long-settled retreats, but are trampled under foot by the shifting throng that forms the population of most of our country places. Besides, there is no encouragement for ghosts in most of our villages, for they have scarcely had time to finish their first nap and turn themselves in their graves before their surviving friends have traveled away from the neighborhood;

so that when they turn out at night to walk their rounds they have no acquaintance left to call upon. This is perhaps the reason why we so seldom hear of ghosts except in our long-established Dutch communities.

The immediate cause, however, of the prevalence of supernatural stories in these parts was doubtless owing to the vicinity of Sleepy Hollow. There was a contagion in the very air that blew from that haunted region; it breathed forth an atmosphere of dreams and fancies infecting all the land. Several of the Sleepy Hollow people were present at Van Tassel's, and, as usual, were doling out their wild and wonderful legends. Many dismal tales were told about funeral trains, and mourning cries and wailings heard and seen about the great tree where the unfortunate Major André was taken, and which stood in the neighborhood. Some mention was made also of the woman in white that haunted the dark glen at Raven Rock, and was often heard to shriek on winter nights before a storm, having perished there in the snow. The chief part of the stories, however, turned upon the favorite specter of Sleepy Hollow, the headless horseman, who had been heard several times of late, patrolling the country, and, it was said, tethered his horse nightly among the graves in the churchyard.

The sequestered situation of this church seems always to have made it a favorite haunt of troubled spirits. It stands on a knoll, surrounded by locust trees and lofty elms, from among which its decent whitewashed walls shine modestly forth, like Christian purity beaming through the shades of retirement. A gentle slope descends from it to a silver sheet of water, bordered by high trees, between which peeps may be caught at the blue hills of the Hudson. To look upon its grass-grown yard, where the sunbeams seem to sleep so quietly, one would think that there at least the dead might rest in peace. On one side of the church extends a wide woody dell, along which raves a large brook among broken rocks and trunks of fallen trees. Over a deep black part of the stream, not far from the church, was formerly thrown a wooden bridge; the road that led to it, and the bridge itself, were thickly shaded by overhanging trees, which cast a gloom about it, even in the daytime, but occasioned a fearful darkness at night. Such was one of the favorite haunts of the headless horseman, and the place where he was most frequently encountered. The tale was told of old Brouwer, a most heretical disbeliever in ghosts, how he met the horseman returning from his foray into Sleepy Hollow, and was obliged to get up behind him; how they galloped over bush and brake, over hill and swamp, until they reached the bridge, when the horseman suddenly turned into a skeleton, threw old Brouwer into the brook, and sprang away over the treetops with a clap of thunder.

This story was immediately matched by a thrice marvelous adventure of Brom Bones, who made light of the galloping Hessian as an arrant jockey. He affirmed that, on returning one night from the neighboring village of Sing Sing, he had been overtaken by this midnight trooper; that he had offered to race with him for a bowl of punch, and should have won it too, for Daredevil beat the goblin horse all hollow, but, just as they came to the church bridge, the Hessian bolted and vanished in a flash of fire.

All these tales, told in that drowsy undertone with

which men talk in the dark, the countenances of the listeners only now and then receiving a casual gleam from the glare of a pipe, sank deep in the mind of Ichabod. He repaid them in kind with large extracts from his invaluable author, Cotton Mather, and added many marvelous events that had taken place in his native State of Connecticut, and fearful sights which he had seen in his nightly walks about Sleepy Hollow.

The revel now gradually broke up. The old farmers gathered together their families in their wagons, and were heard for some time rattling along the hollow roads and over the distant hills. Some of the damsels mounted on pillions behind their favorite swains, and their light-hearted laughter, mingling with the clatter of hoofs, echoed along the silent woodlands, sounding fainter and fainter until they gradually died away—and the late scene of noise and frolic was all silent and deserted. Ichabod only lingered behind, according to the custom of country lovers, to have a tête-à-tête with the heiress, fully convinced that he was now on the high road to success. What passed at this interview I will not pretend to say, for in fact I do not know. Something, however, I fear me, must have gone wrong, for he certainly sallied forth, after no very great interval, with an air quite desolate and chopfallen. Oh these women! these women! Could that girl have been playing off any of her coquettish tricks? Was her encouragement of the poor pedagogue all a mere sham to secure her conquest of his rival? Heaven only knows, not I! Let it suffice to say, Ichabod stole forth with the air of one who had been sacking a hen roost rather than a fair lady's heart. Without looking to the right or left to notice the scene of rural wealth, on which he had so often gloated, he went straight to the stable, and with several hearty cuffs and kicks roused his steed most uncourteously from the comfortable quarters in which he was soundly sleeping, dreaming of mountains of corn and oats, and whole valleys of timothy and clover.

It was the very witching time of night that Ichabod, heavy-hearted and crestfallen, pursued his travel homeward, along the sides of the lofty hills which rise above Tarry Town, and which he had traversed so cheerily in the afternoon. The hour was as dismal as himself. Far below him, the Tappan Zee spread its dusky and indistinct waste of waters, with here and there the tall mast of a sloop, riding quietly at anchor under the land. In the dead hush of midnight he could even hear the barking of the watchdog from the opposite shore of the Hudson, but it was so vague and faint as only to give an idea of his distance from this faithful companion of man. Now and then, too, the long-drawn crowing of a cock, accidentally awakened, would sound far, far off, from some farmhouse away among the hills—but it was like a dreaming sound in his ear. No signs of life occurred near him, but occasionally the melancholy chirp of a cricket, or perhaps the guttural twang of a bullfrog, from a neighboring marsh, as if sleeping uncomfortably and turning suddenly in his bed.

All the stories of ghosts and goblins that he had heard in the afternoon now came crowding upon his recollection. The night grew darker and darker; the stars seemed to sink deeper in the sky, and driving clouds occasionally hid them from his sight. He had never felt so lonely and dismal. He was, moreover,

approaching the very place where many of the scenes
of the ghost stories had been laid. In the center of the
road stood an enormous tulip tree, which towered
like a giant above all the other trees of the neighborhood and formed a kind of landmark. Its limbs were
gnarled and fantastic, large enough to form trunks
for ordinary trees, twisting down almost to the earth
and rising again into the air. It was connected with
the tragical story of the unfortunate André, who had
been taken prisoner hard by; and was universally
known by the name of Major André's tree. The common people regarded it with a mixture of respect and
superstition, partly out of sympathy for the fate of its
ill-starred namesake, and partly from the tales of
strange sights and doleful lamentations told concerning it.

As Ichabod approached this fearful tree, he began
to whistle; he thought his whistle was answered—it
was but a blast sweeping sharply through the dry
branches. As he approached a little nearer, he
thought he saw something white hanging in the
midst of the tree—he paused and ceased whistling;
but on looking more narrowly, perceived that it was a
place where the tree had been scathed by lightning
and the white wood laid bare. Suddenly he heard a
groan—his teeth chattered and his knees smote
against the saddle; it was but the rubbing of one
huge bough upon another as they were swayed about
by the breeze. He passed the tree in safety, but new
perils lay before him.

About two hundred yards from the tree a small
brook crossed the road and ran into a marshy and
thickly wooded glen, known by the name of Wiley's
swamp. A few rough logs, laid side by side, served for

a bridge over this stream. On that side of the road where the brook entered the wood, a group of oaks and chestnuts, matted thick with wild grapevines, threw a cavernous gloom over it. To pass this bridge was the severest trial. It was at this identical spot that the unfortunate André was captured, and under the covert of those chestnuts and vines were the sturdy yeomen concealed who surprised him. This has ever since been considered a haunted stream, and fearful are the feelings of the schoolboy who has to pass it alone after dark.

As he approached the stream his heart began to thump: he summoned up, however, all his resolution, gave his horse half a score of kicks in the ribs, and attempted to dash briskly across the bridge; but instead of starting forward, the perverse old animal made a lateral movement and ran broadside against the fence. Ichabod, whose fears increased with the delay, jerked the reins on the other side, and kicked lustily with the contrary foot; it was all in vain; his steed started, it is true, but it was only to plunge to the opposite side of the road into a thicket of brambles and alder bushes. The schoolmaster now bestowed both whip and heel upon the starveling ribs of old Gunpowder, who dashed forward, snuffling and snorting, but came to a stand just by the bridge with a suddenness that had nearly sent his rider sprawling over his head. Just at this moment a plashy tramp by the side of the bridge caught the sensitive ear of Ichabod. In the dark shadow of the grove, on the margin of the brook, he beheld something huge, misshapen, black and towering. It stirred not, but seemed gathered up in the gloom, like some gigantic monster ready to spring upon the traveler.

The hair of the affrighted pedagogue rose upon his head with terror. What was to be done? To turn and fly was now too late; and besides, what chance was there of escaping ghost or goblin, if such it was, which could ride upon the wings of the wind? Summoning up, therefore, a show of courage, he demanded in stammering accents—"Who are you?" He received no reply. He repeated his demand in a still more agitated voice. Still there was no answer. Once more he cudgeled the sides of the inflexible Gunpowder, and, shutting his eyes, broke forth with involuntary fervor into a psalm tune. Just then the shadowy object of alarm put itself in motion, and, with a scramble and a bound, stood at once in the middle of the road. Though the night was dark and dismal, yet the form of the unknown might now in some degree be ascertained. He appeared to be a horseman of large dimensions, and mounted on a black horse of powerful frame. He made no offer of molestation or sociability, but kept aloof on one side of the road, jogging along on the blind side of old Gunpowder, who had now got over his fright and waywardness.

Ichabod, who had no relish for this strange midnight companion, and bethought himself of the adventure of Brom Bones with the Galloping Hessian, now quickened his steed, in hopes of leaving him behind. The stranger, however, quickened his horse to an equal pace. Ichabod pulled up, and fell into a walk, thinking to lag behind—the other did the same. His heart began to sink within him; he endeavored to resume his psalm tune, but his parched tongue clove to the roof of his mouth, and he could not utter a stave. There was something in the moody and dogged silence of this pertinacious companion

that was mysterious and appalling. It was soon fear-
fully accounted for. On mounting a rising ground,
which brought the figure of his fellow-traveler in relief against the sky, gigantic in height, and muffled in
a cloak, Ichabod was horror-struck on perceiving that
he was headless! But his horror was still more increased on observing that the head, which should
have rested on his shoulders, was carried before him
on the pommel of the saddle. His terror rose to desperation; he rained a shower of kicks and blows upon
Gunpowder, hoping, by a sudden movement, to give
his companion the slip—but the specter started full
jump with him. Away then they dashed, through
thick and thin, stones flying and sparks flashing at
every bound. Ichabod's flimsy garments fluttered in
the air as he stretched his long lank body away over
his horse's head, in the eagerness of his flight.

They had now reached the road which turns off to
Sleepy Hollow; but Gunpowder, who seemed possessed with a demon, instead of keeping up it, made
an opposite turn, and plunged headlong downhill to
the left. This road leads through a sandy hollow,
shaded by trees for about a quarter of a mile, where it
crosses the bridge famous in goblin story, and just beyond swells the green knoll on which stands the
whitewashed church.

As yet the panic of the steed had given his unskillful rider an apparent advantage in the chase; but just
as he had got halfway through the hollow, the girths
of the saddle gave way, and he felt it slipping from
under him. He seized it by the pommel and endeavored to hold it firm, but in vain; and had just time to
save himself by clasping old Gunpowder around the
neck when the saddle fell to the earth, and he heard

it trampled under foot by his pursuer. For a moment the terror of Hans Van Ripper's wrath passed across his mind—for it was his Sunday saddle; but this was no time for petty fears; the goblin was hard on his haunches, and (unskillful rider that he was!) he had much ado to maintain his seat, sometimes slipping on one side, sometimes on the other, and sometimes jolted on the high ridge of his horse's backbone with a violence that he verily feared would cleave him asunder.

An opening in the trees now cheered him with the hopes that the church bridge was at hand. The wavering reflection of a silver star in the bosom of the brook told him that he was not mistaken. He saw the walls of the church dimly glaring under the trees beyond. He recollected the place where Brom Bones's ghostly competitor had disappeared. "If I can but reach that bridge," thought Ichabod, "I am safe." Just then he heard the black steed panting and blowing close behind him; he even fancied that he felt his hot breath. Another convulsive kick in the ribs and old Gunpowder sprang upon the bridge; he thundered over the resounding planks; he gained the opposite side; and now Ichabod cast a look behind to see if his pursuer should vanish, according to rule, in a flash of fire and brimstone. Just then he saw the goblin rising in his stirrups, and in the very act of hurling his head at him. Ichabod endeavored to dodge the horrible missile, but too late. It encountered his cranium with a tremendous crash—he was tumbled headlong into the dust, and Gunpowder, the black steed, and the goblin rider, passed by like a whirlwind.

The next morning the old horse was found without his saddle, and with the bridle under his feet, soberly cropping the grass at his master's gate. Ichabod did not make his appearance at breakfast—dinner hour came, but no Ichabod. The boys assembled at the schoolhouse, and strolled idly about the banks of the brook; but no schoolmaster. Hans Van Ripper now began to feel some uneasiness about the fate of poor Ichabod, and his saddle. An inquiry was set on foot, and after diligent investigation they came upon his traces. In one part of the road leading to the church was found the saddle trampled in the dirt; the tracks of horses' hoofs deeply dented in the road, and evidently at furious speed, were traced to the bridge, beyond which, on the bank of a broad part of the brook, where the water ran deep and black, was found the hat of the unfortunate Ichabod, and close beside it a shattered pumpkin.

The brook was searched, but the body of the schoolmaster was not to be discovered. Hans Van Ripper, as executor of his estate, examined the bundle which contained all his worldly effects. They consisted of two shirts and a half, two stocks for the neck, a pair or two of worsted stockings, an old pair of corduroy small clothes, a rusty razor, a book of psalm tunes full of dogs' ears, and a broken pitchpipe. As to the books and furniture of the schoolhouse, they belonged to the community, excepting Cotton Mather's *History of Witchcraft, a New England Almanac,* and a book of dreams and fortune-telling; in which last was a sheet of foolscap much scribbled and blotted in several fruitless attempts to make a copy of verses in honor of the heiress of Van Tassel. These magic books and the poetic scrawl were forthwith consigned to the flames by Hans Van Ripper, who from that time forward determined to send his children no more to school, observing that he never knew any good come of this same reading and writing. Whatever money the schoolmaster possessed, and he had received his quarter's pay but a day or two before, he must have had about his person at the time of his disappearance.

The mysterious event caused much speculation at the church on the following Sunday. Knots of gazers and gossips were collected in the churchyard, at the bridge, and at the spot where the hat and pumpkin had been found. The stories of Brouwer, of Bones, and a whole budget of others were called to mind; and when they had diligently considered them all and compared them with the symptoms of the present case, they shook their heads and came to the conclusion that Ichabod had been carried off by the galloping Hessian. As he was a bachelor and in nobody's debt, nobody troubled his head any more about him. The school was removed to a different quarter of the hollow, and another pedagogue reigned in his stead.

It is true an old farmer, who had been down to New York on a visit several years after, and from whom this account of the ghostly adventure was received, brought home the intelligence that Ichabod Crane was still alive; that he had left the neighborhood, partly through fear of the goblin and Hans Van Ripper, and partly in mortification at having been suddenly dismissed by the heiress; that he had changed his quarters to a distant part of the country, had kept school and studied law at the same time, had been admitted to the bar, turned politician, electioneered, written for the newspapers, and finally had been made a justice of the Ten Pound Court. Brom Bones too, who shortly after his rival's disappearance conducted the blooming Katrina in triumph to the altar, was observed to look exceedingly knowing whenever the story of Ichabod was related, and always burst into a hearty laugh at the mention of the pumpkin, which led some to suspect that he knew more about the matter than he chose to tell.

The old country wives, however, who are the best judges of these matters, maintain to this day that Ichabod was spirited away by supernatural means; and it is a favorite story often told about the neighborhood around the winter evening fire. The bridge became more than ever an object of superstitious awe, and that may be the reason why the road has been altered of late years, so as to approach the church by the border of the millpond. The schoolhouse, being deserted, soon fell to decay, and was reported to be haunted by the ghost of the unfortunate pedagogue; and the plowboy, loitering homeward of a still summer evening, has often fancied his voice at a distance, chanting a melancholy psalm tune among the tranquil solitudes of Sleepy Hollow.

POSTSCRIPT

Found in the Handwriting of Mr. Knickerbocker

The preceding Tale is given, almost in the precise words in which I heard it related at a Corporation meeting of the ancient city of Manhattoes, at which were present many of its sagest and most illustrious burghers. The narrator was a pleasant, shabby, gentlemanly old fellow, in pepper-and-salt clothes, with a sadly humorous face, and one whom I strongly suspected of being poor—he made such efforts to be entertaining. When his story was concluded, there was much laughter and approbation, particularly from two or three deputy aldermen, who had been asleep a greater part of the time. There was, however, one tall, dry-looking old gentleman with beetling eyebrows, who maintained a grave and rather severe face throughout, now and then folding his arms, inclining his head, and looking down upon the floor, as if turning a doubt over in his mind. He was one of your wary men, who never laugh but upon good grounds—when they have reason and the law on their side. When the mirth of the rest of the company had subsided and silence was restored, he leaned one arm on the elbow of his chair, and, sticking the other akimbo, demanded, with a slight but exceedingly sage motion of the head, and contraction of the brow, what was the moral of the story, and what it went to prove?

The storyteller, who was just putting a glass of wine to his lips as a refreshment after his toils, paused for a moment, looked at his inquirer with an air of infinite deference, and, lowering the glass slowly to the table, observed that the story was intended most logically to prove:

"That there is no situation in life but has its advantages and pleasures—provided we will but take a joke as we find it.

"That, therefore, he that runs races with goblin troopers is likely to have rough riding of it."

"Ergo, for a country schoolmaster to be refused the hand of a Dutch heiress is a certain step to high preferment in the state."

The cautious old gentleman knit his brows tenfold

closer after this explanation, being sorely puzzled by the ratiocination of the syllogism; while, methought, the one in pepper-and-salt eyed him with something of a triumphant leer. At length, he observed, that all this was very well, but still he thought the story a little on the extravagant—there were one or two points on which he had his doubts.

"Faith, sir," replied the storyteller, "as to that matter, I don't believe one-half of it myself."

D.K.

ABOUT PETER LERANGIS

PETER LERANGIS is the author of the popular book series Watchers (www.morphz.com/watchers/) as well as two best-selling teen horror novels, *The Yearbook* and *Driver's Dead,* and many other books for young readers, including *It Came from the Cafeteria* and *Attack of the Killer Potatoes.* His new two-book series, Antarctica, will be published in fall 2000. He lives in New York City, due south of Sleepy Hollow, with his wife, Tina deVaron, and their two sons.

ABOUT
WASHINGTON IRVING

Best known today as the creator of Rip Van Winkle, Ichabod Crane, and the Headless Horseman, WASHINGTON IRVING enjoyed a varied career as lawyer, businessman, diplomat, and writer. Born April 3, 1783, in New York City, he was the youngest of eight surviving children of a Scottish father and an English mother. When Irving was six years old, his nurse saw President George Washington in a shop and persuaded him to bless his namesake. It was the first of Irving's many associations with American presidents. In his teenage years Irving became familiar with the area of the Hudson River north of New York City, a part of the state that later was to figure importantly in his writings. Although Irving went to work in a law office, his interest soon turned to writing, and in 1802 he began publishing letters under the pen name Jonathan Oldstyle, Gent. In 1804 Irving was sent to Europe for his health. His ship was robbed by pirates, and for the next two years Irving socialized with the Americans and English abroad before returning home in 1806. He resumed his work in the law office but also continued to write, co-authoring *Salmagundi* (1807–8) and creating the fictional author Diedrich Knickerbocker, whose *A History of New York* was published in 1809 to instant success. In 1817, in London, Irving started work on *The Sketch Book of Geoffrey Crayon, Gent.*, which included the story "The Legend of Sleepy Hollow." The

Sketch Book was published in the United States in seven installments in 1819. Seven years later Irving went to Spain as the attaché to the American legation in Madrid, although he had no official duties. During that time he wrote a biography of Christopher Columbus and visited southern Spain, which inspired him to write *The Alhambra* (tales and sketches). In 1832 he returned home and settled in the Hudson River valley, eventually buying a cottage (which he named Sunnyside) and ten acres along the river, two miles south of Tarrytown. There he enjoyed the company of his large family of nieces and nephews. He continued to write, and he continued his involvement in political life. In 1842 President John Tyler appointed him minister to Spain during a time of political turmoil. He resigned the position in 1845 and returned home a year later. Although his health was not good, he worked on a biography of George Washington (eventually comprising five volumes) and revised earlier works. By 1856 Irving rarely left Sunnyside, although he continued to receive visitors. He died there on November 28, 1859.